# PROFESSOR MAGNETO
## and his
# AMAZING MECHANICAL MAN

A Short Story Collection

by Joe Gillespie

# PROFESSOR MAGNETO
## and his
# AMAZING MECHANICAL MAN

By Joe Gillespie

© 2017 Joe Gillespie

ISBN: 9780993526596

Arkbound is a social enterprise that aims to promote social
inclusion, community development and artistic talent. It
sponsors publications by disadvantaged authors and covers
issues that engage wider social concerns. Arkbound fully
embraces sustainability and environmental protection. It
endeavours to use material that is renewable, recyclable or
sourced from sustainable forest.

Arkbound
Backfields House
Upper York Street
Bristol BS2 8QJ
England

www.arkbound.com

*For Maevis, Oscar and Edgar*

# Table of Contents

# Foreword

In 1979 I was working for a company in London's Soho district. In my lunch hour, I would usually go to one of two excellent sandwich bars in Wardour Street and would pass through an alleyway called St. Anne's Court.

On one side of the alley were a number of doors with red lights over them. The dingy stairways led to ... I never found out. On the other side of the alleyway was a shop called 'Dark They Were and Golden-Eyed', a reference to a short story by Ray Bradbury. It was Europe's largest science fiction bookshop.

Most days, I would spend twenty minutes, or so browsing the great many books and magazines on offer. There were paperbacks, fanzines, graphic novels, comics and all kinds of fascinating items. It was rare that I came out of that shop without one or two paperbacks in my hand.

My journey into central London each morning was on a Number 9 bus. It was fortunate that the bus station was at the end of the short cul-de-sac where I lived. The advantage of getting onto an empty bus in the morning meant that I had the pick of all the seats. I chose the front seat, on the right hand side, on the top deck. There I would be relatively undisturbed, and would have half an hour of peace to write.

At first, I used pen and paper. Later, I had a Tandy laptop with its two-inch-high, black and white LCD screen.

I wrote science fiction short stories. I loved the longer books by Isaac Asimov, Arthur C. Clarke and, especially, Larry Niven – but I read those in the evenings. On the morning bus ride my mind was clear and I wrote.

Many of the stories I wrote back then are lost in the mists of time, probably due a massive clear-out before having building work done on the house. When I eventually left that house all of my notebooks and folders were crammed into boxes by the removal men and ended up in my new home's large attic.

It was with great delight that I opened one of these boxes one day recently, looking for something else, and found this time capsule from a younger me in the past: a loose-leaf folder, a couple of ring-bound notebooks and a number of short stories. Some were typed on the Tandy laptop and printed out, others were hastily scribbled on a shaking omnibus. I had very good handwriting at early school but in later years it diminished due to the rapid scrawling of notes in science classes.

Although there are a few newer stories in this collection, the majority were written some thirty-five years ago. They were directly influenced by the books I was reading back then; the books of what I consider to be the golden age of science fiction.

Now, I have a confession to make. I have had to make a few minor changes to these stories. Science has a nasty habit of catching up with fiction!

Although the science fiction short story has all but disappeared, they are in a unique position to communicate sharp new ideas and expound concepts without the waffle that so often accompanies modern novels.

I now cordially invite you, dear reader, to come and join me in this expedition across space and time.

*Joe Gillespie, 1st November 2016*

# Professor Magneto
## and his
# Amazing Mechanical Man

Splosh!

Jack Willard held a rolled-up circus flyer under his chin and slapped a hefty dollop of paste onto the old wooden fence. The fence had been long-used for such announcements; the old ones were seldom removed and recorded a history of shows and events going back for many years. Using the same long-handled brush, Jack smoothed out the fly-poster alongside three others – all identical.

'Roget's Circus,' it proclaimed. 'All the thrills of the Big Top starring The Amazing Vincentis: Daring-do on the Trapeze and High Wire.'

'The Great Lorenzo: Fire Eater and Sword Swallower extraordinaire.'

'The Spectacular Roget's Liberty Horses.'

'Roll in laughter to the antics of Koko the Clown and his pals, Stumpy and Jacques.'

The gaudy poster displayed a collage of the circus acts in fanciful poses and dubious situations – more idealistic that representative. A panel at the bottom was overprinted with the times, location and admission prices.

Jack stood back, admired his handiwork, and tossed his brush and paste bucket into the open back of his rusty old pick-up truck.

He jumped into the cab, slammed the door and headed off to the next location.

A large 4x4 towing a shiny silver trailer pulled into the grassy field gouged with tyre marks of heavy vehicles in the soft ground. It had been raining and there was the heady smell of wet grass.

The shiny aluminium trailer was just like any regular Airstream travel trailer except that it had a peculiar fin growing out of the top and two vestigial wings on either side. Moisture cascaded down the sides, forming rivulets in the mirrored metal surface.

A tall, thin figure swung out of the cab and landed on the flattened wet grass with a squelch.

"Who's boss around here?" he called, trying to make himself heard over the din of a diesel generator.

A short, stout man in a brown Stetson and leather jacket broke off from a group of others deep in discussion and wandered over to him.

"Theo Rogers," he offered his hand. "Theodore Rogers the Third."

"What can I do for you?"

The taller man looked round at the circle of brightly-painted trucks and trailers and the red and cream circus tent still being erected.

"I was kind of hoping that we might be of use to each other," he said, rocking back on his heels a little. "Fact is; I'm looking to team up with an outfit like yours."

Theo detected a hint of a foreign accent but couldn't quite place it. East European perhaps? Russian? He frowned.

"Oh really, what you got?"

"Call myself Professor Magneto," came the reply, "and I have this, um, mechanical man."

"Mechanical man?" questioned Theo.

He blinked. In all his time in the circus and going back three generations, he had never heard tell of a mechanical man in a circus act.

Magneto could sense that the man was uncomfortable with the concept.

"Allow me to show you please," he begged, beckoning Theo toward his trailer as he headed towards it.

He grabbed the handle and opened the door. Reaching inside, he pulled a small box from the interior. It looked like a model airplane radio-control transmitter but seemed to have a lot more knobs and switches than usual. He flicked one of the switches, twisted a knob, and then another.

The door to the trailer framed a silvery metal figure with glowing violet eyes.

"This is Charlie," explained Magneto, twisting his mouth.

Charlie looked more like Dorothy's Tin-Man than a hi-tech robot. It looked like it had been jury-rigged from pieces of junk.

"Charlie is my amazing mechanical man and he can perform just about any circus act you like. You name it, he can do it."

"Oh yeh," sighed the boss. "Now I've heard everything."

"Look, we ain't hiring at the minute," he hissed. "Things are a bit…" he rocked his hands, "…quiet at the minute. Can't do anything for you, fella. Sorry."

"Tell you what," said Magneto, waving a pair of jazz hands vigorously. "Give me a try-out, it won't cost you anything. If you like what you see, maybe we talk some more?"

Theo stroked his chin and looked back at Charlie.

"Mmm. Let me think about it."

"Aw, come on Vince," complained the pretty young woman in the spangled leotard. "Take it easy on the booze."

"Just to steady my hands," the young man replied wiping his sleeve across his mouth and slipping the hip-flask into his back pocket.

Dorrie had just turned twenty-four. She had blonde hair pulled-up into a short pony tail and the lithe figure of an athlete. She was Theo and Marie's daughter. Her real name was Doreen but she hated it. That was the name her Mother used when scolding her as a child.

She was born into to the circus exhibiting a natural ability for circus skills from a very early age. Like her sister Polly, she was an all-rounder, walking the high wire, swinging from a trapeze and performing death-defying gymnastics on the back of a galloping pony. She had sawdust in her blood.

Vince was a little older. As a disillusioned teenager and college dropout, he had run away from home to join the circus. He started-off mucking-out the animals and doing odd jobs, but Dorrie had taken a shine to him and schooled him in the ways of the circus. He was a good pupil.

Vince was now the resident knife thrower and

the other half of the star trapeze act, 'The Vincentis', but like many other circus folk, Vince and Dorrie had multiple roles. A quick costume change and they were transformed into a different act entirely.

"Vince, it's me that's at the receiving end of your knife throwing. Just lay off the alcohol or you'll have to find yourself another pin-cushion!"

"Have I ever as much as split a hair on your pretty little locks?" asked Vince in exasperation.

The couple's tiff was interrupted by Polly stepping up into the trailer, her tall ostrich feather headdress brushing the top of the door.

"Hey, you guys. Heard about the new act in town?"

She pulled Dorrie over to the doorway and pointed at the silver trailer across the way.

Vince joined them, putting his arms over the two girls' shoulders. Polly pushed him off with a scowl.

"What's that all about?" asked Vince.

"Professor Magneto and his Amazing Mechanical Man," chimed Polly. "Pop's giving him a trial tonight. Should be interesting."

"Ugh Vince, I can smell the booze on your breath!"

Vince gave her a pat on the butt and got a smack round the head from Dorrie. He stepped out of the door and headed over to the silver trailer followed by the two girls.

Vince tapped on the door of the odd-looking trailer.

No reply.

He knocked again, a bit more forcefully. The door cracked slightly.

"Who's there? What do you want?" came a sharp voice from inside.

"Oh, just came to say 'Hi'," called Vince.

The door opened a little more and a tall man walked out and stood on the trailer step, deliberately pulling the door behind him. He was handsome, too handsome. The kind of handsome you only get on catwalks and in fashion magazines: tall cheekbones and black hair sleeked back with hair cream. He looked like he was in his late thirties and was clad only in a black dressing gown.

"Just came to say 'Hi'," repeated Vince. The two girls behind him waved cutely.

Magneto nodded slowly in acknowledgement but remained silent.

"So, whatcha doin' in these parts?" asked Vince.

"Work," came the blunt reply.

Vince looked at the girls for a reaction but they just stared blankly.

"You performing tonight then?" asked Vince expectantly.

Magneto nodded again.

"What exactly is it that you do?" quizzed Dorrie.

"You'll see," replied Magneto slipping back inside the trailer and careful to block any glimpse of the interior.

The door shut with a soft metallic click.

"Weird," whispered Polly slowly.

Theo, The Ringmaster, held up his hands to quieten the crowd and waited until the noise abated.

He held out his arm.

"And now, Ladies and Gentlemen, for the very first time with Roget's Circus, let me introduce you to Professor Magneto and his Amazing Mechanical Man."

They clapped.

A tall, slim figure in a silver lamé jumpsuit walked into the ring followed by two men pushing a tall silver box on wheels. Magneto wore a close-fitting silver skull cap with little art deco wings covering his ears and looking like some comic book hero from the 1950s. Hanging from a chord around his neck, he grasped a remote control box with two spinning antennae. One came out of the top and the other from the side.

He flicked a switch and the sides of the box collapsed to the ground, accompanied by a just-a-little-too-late cymbal crash.

Donny, the drummer, wasn't a great timekeeper at the best of times but this was the first time he had seen this act – which didn't help.

"Charlie, the Amazing Mechanical Man," shouted Magneto, raising his hand in the air.

He passed his hand over the controls and Charlie's eyes lit up to an intense violet glow. Charlie's head rotated a full three hundred and sixty degrees and he bowed to polite applause.

A large, pearl ball rolled out into the ring.

Charlie moved over to the ball in a series of spasmodic jerks and scrambled up on top. He stood upright, wiggling a little as he got his balance. Slowly, the ball rolled round the ring, with Charlie teetering on top as the spotlight followed him.

There were hoots of laughter from the audience.

Standing outside the ring in the shadows, Theo and Marie looked at each other.

Theo grimaced.

Marie shrugged.

Magneto pulled a seesaw into the spotlight. Charlie manipulated the rolling ball up one side, balanced for a few seconds on top, and rolled slowly down the other side.

More polite clapping.

Theo raised his eyebrows, sighed and shook his head.

Marie looked back at him. "Hey, give the guy a chance," she insisted.

Charlie was back down off the seesaw and standing on one leg rocking the ball backwards and forwards on the spot.

Magneto walked over and, with a hefty kick, knocked the large ball away to the edge of the ring.

Charlie stayed fixed in the air where he had been, four feet off the ground.

Gasps of astonishment came from the crowd.

Donny decided that it would be a good time for a cymbal crash.

Charlie put his two arms out horizontally and

turned to Lorenzo's knife-throwing wheel. He concentrated hard on the five knives still sticking into the wood. One by one, they came away, whipping across and sticking to his body with loud clanks.

The crowd went wild.

Finally, with his arms still wide in mid-air, he did a quick spin and helicoptered slowly to the ground.

Magneto held his arm up towards Charlie, who took a stiff bow, and they moved off towards the tunnel.

The Ringmaster strode in with his arms aloft and then went towards the exiting duo.

"Let me hear it for Professor Magneto and his truly Amazing Mechanical Man," he shouted.

The house was in uproar.

Several towns later, Marie Rogers was neatening a wad of bills, tapping them this way and that on the table in front of her. She stretched a rubber band around them and stacked them with others.

She was a short woman of indeterminate middle age with blonde hair – although her roots disagreed. The half-smoked cigarette stuck to her bright red lipstick that went just a little too far beyond the lips.

"How's it looking?" quizzed Theo, with a look of anticipation.

"Not bad. Not bad at all," smiled Marie.

"Things are certainly looking up at last, thanks to your new prodigy and his funky tin puppet."

Theo scowled.

"Don't let Magneto hear you calling his mechanical man a tin puppet. That is a miracle of engineering!"

Marie shook her head slowly.

"That guy sure gives me the heebie-jeebies," she muttered.

"Well," responded Theo, "He keeps himself to himself, sure, but I think he's harmless enough and you can't deny he's done wonders for the bottom line! A few months ago, I was ready to pack it all in. Sell up the lot. And who in his right mind would buy a flea-bitten outfit like this?"

He waved his arm across the interior of the trailer.

"Time was when a circus had real excitement. Exotic animals – lions, tigers, elephants, bears. We can't afford all that – even if they weren't banned by the animal rights crowd. All we have is a few ponies and assortment of mangy pooches."

Sure enough, Roger's Travelling Circus had started-off as a grand affair: four rings, great acts, and a bright future.

Theo's father, Theodore Rogers II, took over when the old man took ill ... but he had an expensive habit called poker. He died at an early age and the circus, or what was left of it, was passed-on to his son, Theo III. Theo liked poker too, but he made a point of never playing for money. He used matchsticks.

Theo tried his best to get the circus back on its feet but it was like pushing water uphill. Marie convinced him to rename it "Roget's Circus" because it sounded more up-market and distanced it, to some degree, from his father's bad reputation.

Animal rights movements had come down hard on the import and exploitation of wild animals. Health and safety legislation tamed the more dangerous stunts to half-hearted parodies. Audience numbers dropped away dramatically.

"Magneto is pulling them in and I think we are very lucky that he hooked up with us," breathed Theo.

"Humph," shrugged the woman.

"I have the strangest feeling about that guy!"

Brian hefted up the steps into the clown's trailer as best as his short legs could manage.

Koko and Jacques had already done their makeup.

Koko was a pierrot with a white baggy costume, a big ruffle and a conical hat. Jacques wore black dungarees and a French blue and white striped t-shirt and a trilby sitting on a mop of multi-coloured hair.

"Better get a move on, Brian," said Koko pointing to a high chair in front of a small mirror surrounded by naked light bulbs.

"Plenty of time," barked Brian. "I've done this before, you know, Shmuck!"

He lifted a jar of white greasepaint and rubbed some on his face. With a fat, red make-up stick, he drew-on a wide smile. Using a smaller black pencil, he outlined the smile and put a cross over each eye. A shiny red ball was clipped over his nose. He pulled-on a small black hat with a large plastic daisy sticking out of the hat band.

"There," he said, "what's the panic?"

"You going on like that?" asked Jacques, looking down at Brian's t-shirt and jeans.

"Oh!" exclaimed the midget, pulling his loud checked suit down from a coat hanger.

"Be right with you."

Brian pulled-on the suit and did-up the buttons. He swung round in front of a long mirror and brushed at his shoulder.

"There you are. 'Stumpy the Clown'. At your service!"

Stan (saxophone), LeRoy (trumpet), Ken (trombone) and Donny (drums) sat on the bandstand. Of them all, Donny had the hardest job. Apart from providing the rhythm for the circus band, he had to produce all the drum rolls, cymbal crashes and general sound effects for the entire show, which he did with aplomb – if never quite on time.

Theo and Marie, dressed in their guises of Ringmaster and Ring mistress, swept into the ring with a flourish.

Theo was decked in a top hat and wore a large black cape over a red and gold coat. His shirt was white and frilly and in his right hand he held a long whip. His drawn-on pencil moustache gave him an air of elegance – aided by a very tight corset to tame his slack, middle age spread.

Marie wore much the same attire but didn't seem

to be so concerned by her ample proportions. She removed Theo's cape, tossed it behind the bandstand, and bowed to the audience.

"Ladies and Gentlemen. Boys and Girls. Let us welcome you, this fine evening, to the sensational, the spectacular, the one and only, Roget's Circus."

The band started playing 'March of the Gladiators' but with only three instruments it sounded insipid.

From the tunnel, the three clowns came tumbling in – somersaulting, doing cartwheels, falling over and generally slapping sticks.

The crowd laughed and cheered.

Theo cracked his whip and immediately four white ponies came galloping into the ring. Polly was standing on top of the lead pony swirling streamers wildly with both hand.

Round and round they went.

Polly tossed the streamers to the ground, leaned over and put her hands flat on her pony's back. She lifted one leg high into the air and steadied herself. After another circuit of the ring, she raised her other leg to form a perfect handstand.

The crowd clapped in appreciation.

Polly then moved her left arm out to the side gingerly so that she was balanced entirely on one arm.

Greater applause.

After a few more laps of the ring, she returned to her standing position, arms outstretched, and did a backflip somersault. The cymbals crashed and the ponies trotted back out of the ring.

Drum roll.

The Ringmaster tossed his whip to the side and threw his head back.

"Ladies and Gentlemen, give a warm welcome to The Great Lorenzo!" He held his arm out to the side to indicate the entrance of Vince on a unicycle wearing a Gypsy costume and juggling with three flaming torches.

Much clapping.

Vince, or 'The Great Lorenzo', hopped off the unicycle without missing a beat in his juggling. He threw the torches high in the air and, as they came back down, caught them with one hand. He then ran the flames up and down his muscular arms before extinguishing them, one by one, in his mouth.

Dorrie ran into the ring wearing a bright scarlet one-piece and matching lipstick. Her resemblance to a young Marilyn Monroe was not unintentional as she pouted and blew kisses to the crowd. She spun a large wooden wheel with a spiral painted on it,- stopped it and then stood hard against the wood.

Lorenzo produced a handful of large throwing knives from a shoulder bag and, in a series of smooth flowing movements, placed each one just inches away from Dorrie's semi-clad body.

The crowd gasped.

Lorenzo bowed and held out his arm towards Dorrie.

Applause.

He walked over to the wheel and extracted the

knives from the woodwork. Dorrie spread-eagled herself against the wheel and Lorenzo tied her wrists, ankles and waist to the contraption and gave it a spin. Theo stepped up and kept the wheel spinning as Lorenzo retreated with his knives aloft.

Drum roll.

He turned round. Slowly and deliberately he flung each knife at the spinning target, pausing slightly between each throw to take aim. As each knife hit the wheel inches away from Dorrie, there was a cymbal crash.

Lorenzo went over and brought the wheel to a halt. He loosened Dorrie's ties and she stepped forward with her arms in the air to a rapturous applause. Lorenzo and Dorrie bowed several times and ran off into the tunnel to a quick-tempoed circus galop from the band.

Polly stroked her favourite pony, Nimbus, and fed him a carrot. She led him over to the canvas enclosure where the other ponies grazed and took him in. Beside the corral was an archway with an illuminated sign over it. "Roget's Circus Sideshows."

Big Jeff, the circus strongman, stepped onto his platform from the back with an armful of dumbbells and set them down. Had they been made of real iron, and not wood painted to look like iron, he could never have done that. He wiped his hands and straightened-up a metal stand that held a bag of powdered chalk.

Earlier, Jeff had been one of the small team that erected the big top. He was big, and strong – but not that strong. He helped unload the canvas from the flat truck and rolled it out into position on the ground. An electric winch on the front of a large tractor unit did all the hard work. With the four king-poles in place, the heavy canvas tent was winched-up and the queen poles hefted into place by the circus grunts.

Now, he had a show to put on.

Jeff opened the red curtains that covered the front of the platform and peered out along the sideshow aisle. Other curiosities were setting-up their pitches.

Madam Mona, the fortune teller, unfolded an ornate, oriental cloth and spread it out over a small table in her tent. She removed a glass ball from a mahogany box, polished it, and set it on a small black circular stand in the centre of the table. She unrolled a Persian rug and placed it on the floor -careful to cover up the electrical cables that ran from under the table to devices hidden behind the red and gold wall hangings. She was all set.

The flap of her tent opened and a very small man walked in.

"Hi Brian," she said. Isn't it time to get yourself ready?"

He shook his head from side to side.

"Have you seen a chicken running around anywhere?" said the midget. "Lou's chicken got out and it's run off."

Mona chuckled.

"You mean the two-headed chicken?" said Mona raising her voice at the end of the sentence.

"Yes … No." squeaked Brian. "It hasn't had its second head fitted-on yet. Lou has started panicking. Chickens can't disappear into thin air like that."

"I'll watch out for it," smiled Mona unconvincingly.

Down the canvas alleyway, Bud wrestled with his baggy dress, pulling it on over his black leggings. He pulled the dress down all round and adjusted the straps of his voluminous brassiere. From a cardboard box, he took out a black curly wig and pulled it over his bald head. Looking in a hand mirror, he straightened the wig, combing it to tease the curls back into place. With the same comb, he tidied-up his bushy black beard.

Brian came running past with a chicken under his arm that was clucking furiously, feathers flying.

"The show must go on!" he yelled, disappearing behind a red and cream striped awning.

"Lou. Lou…"

From the other end of the alley, a girl appeared with three dogs on leads. The Jack Russell had a little black coat and a bowtie. The Spaniel, a cloth saddle with a tiny monkey sitting on it. The French Poodle wore a tutu and silver collar studded with rhinestones. They twisted past one another.

Brian came out from behind the awning, wiping his forearm across his forehead.

"Hi Tracy," he shouted to the dog handler and skipped off towards the trailer with clowns painted on the sides.

Vince and Dorrie had changed into their 'Vincentis' costumes and were waiting in the tunnel to go on for their high wire act.

As Magneto and Charlie passed by, The Vincentis gave a little silent applause.

"How the Hell did you do that?" asked Vince.

Magneto looked him up and down slowly and then over at Dorrie.

He tapped his nose.

Taking Dorrie by the hand, he peered closely at a nasty cut on her arm and looked over at Vince accusingly.

"Just a scratch," smiled Vince, taking a good swig from his hip flask. "Goes with the job. She'll get over it."

Magneto held up Dorrie's arm to Charlie.

"Charlie," he said.

Charlie's eyes grew brighter and brighter and two beams of violet light criss-crossed over Dorrie's wound. There was a gentle hum. Miraculously, the cut healed over and dissolved into clear, healthy skin.

Vince's jaw dropped. He pointed at the site of the cut and tried to speak – but couldn't.

Dorrie rubbed her arm.

"Thank you, Charlie," she said under her breath. "Thank you very much."

The band started up The Vincenti's entrance music.

As they ran out into the ring, Dorrie looked back, but Magneto and Charlie were gone.

The snare drum rolled as they mounted the metal-runged rope ladder and climbed high into the apex of the big top.

They performed their death-defying high wire act to much appreciation from the crowd.

Another day, another show.

Vince searched the trailer for his hidden bottle. There was no sign of it. Either he had forgotten where he had hidden it, which was very unlikely as he only had three hidey-holes, or someone had taken it. He could guess who.

The circus was pitched on the outskirts of the small town of Truville. Vince needed a drink. He pulled-on his coat and wandered off into the night.

"Haven't seen you around these parts before," said the barkeep of the nearly empty bar.

"No, I'm not from round here," replied Vince.

"Are you with the circus, then?" suggested the barkeep.

"Yeh, what of it?" snapped Vince.

"Oh, nuthin'," came the reply. "Just bein' nosey. What's your poison?"

"Whiskey," said Vince. "Double."

Vince hauled himself onto a stool and took long sips. His mind was miles away.

"I hear you have some weird mechanical man act. Folks are talking about it," said the man polishing the glass. "What's the gimmick?"

Vince shrugged.

"Come and see for yourself."

"Can't. I'm stuck here every night," sighed the barkeep.

"Mmm," said Vince. "Professor Magneto and his Amazing Mechanical Man. That's what it says on the poster."

He pushed his empty glass toward the barkeep and nodded at it. It was topped-up.

"Gimmick? I don't know," said Vince. "He just turned-up one day and persuaded the boss to give him a job. Don't know anything about him. Haven't spoken more than two words to him, or him to me."

"All sounds a bit suspicious," said the barkeep with raised eyebrows.

"Aw, he seems harmless enough," said Vince.

"And what do you do?" asked the barkeep.

"Hold the whole thing together," slurred Vince. "Not an easy job."

"I wanted to join a circus when I was a boy," proffered the barkeep.

"Then why didn't you?" asked Vince.

The barkeep grinned.

"Couldn't do nuthin'."

"That's what stops most people," said Vince. "They all think it is a glamorous life. It's not. It's nine months of hauling around from one dead-end town to another. Up at the crack of dawn. Backbreaking work to pitch the tent, feed the animals. There is no glamour anywhere."

Vince sat thinking and shaking his head.

"Don't know how much longer I'm going to stick it."

The barkeep was now polishing the bar top.

"Hey, can you give me a half bottle to go?" said Vince, pointing at the rows of bottles behind the bar.

"Sure," said the barkeep, "but it will be a lot cheaper if you go across the road to the grocery store."

"If I don't care then you don't care," said Vince pushing a bill across the bar.

He pushed the bottle into his jacket inside pocket, lifted his hand in thanks and walked out like someone trying very hard to look sober.

Word soon got around about Professor Magneto and his Amazing Mechanical Man.

People at work talked about him.

Kids at school talked about him.

Long lines flowed away from the ticket trailer every night in every town. Roget's Circus had to run two evening shows to get them all in. One started at 5:30 and a second at 7:30.

Polly had to join Marie selling the tickets. In her usual place at the entrance, Koko and Jacques took the tickets from the customers while Stumpy showed them in with his funny little waddle.

Magneto became the headline act and Theo had to

commission new flyers featuring the pair.

Takings were up over three hundred percent!

Theo and Marie splashed-out on a swanky new trailer, passing their old one to Polly and her new love interest, Jack Thompson – Jacques the Clown.

Late one evening, Theo, Marie, Vince and Dorrie, Polly and Jack were sitting in the new trailer playing cards and having a celebratory drink.

"Did nobody think to ask Magneto?" asked Jack.

"Didn't want to come," replied Theo. "Likes his own company better."

"He always has Charlie," quipped Dorrie.

"Yes, that relationship worries me," smirked Vince.

They all giggled.

"No, he's watching tv," said Marie pointing out the window at Magneto's trailer, where a bluish light flickered on the blind.

"He doesn't have a television," contradicted Vince, "no dish."

"Don't know about you," he continued, "I find him a bit creepy. What do you know about him, Theo?"

Theo poured himself another whiskey and handed the bottle to Vince. He leaned back into his soft new seat and squeezed his lips tightly together thoughtfully.

"His papers say he's Ivan Pavlov. Got a degree in some sort of engineering from a university somewhere I've never heard of."

"Who cares," he went on, "he's turned this show

into a little gold mine, that's all that matters."

Marie put her hand on his knee.

"And he don't look so bad either," she winked.

They all played matchstick poker, drank and laughed into the early hours.

Next night, the band were playing a fanfare as Magneto stepped into the spotlight to great applause. This is who the crowd had really come to see.

He spun on his heels and held out his left arm towards the tall box that had just been wheeled in.

The snare drum rolled.

A puff of smoke and a cymbal crash and there was Charlie standing to attention.

A great cheer came from the crowd.

Magneto raised his hand for quiet and the crowd hushed.

"Tonight, Ladies and Gentlemen, we try something a little different."

Charlie climbed onto his big white ball and did a couple of laps of the ring. He did his usual seesaw routine impeccably but instead of helicoptering to the ground, as he always did, he left the ball at the end of the seesaw and jumped off it onto the other end. The large ball shot up into the air high above the ring – and just stayed there.

There were gasps from the audience.

Charlie raised his arms, pointing at the ball, and directed it to float down slowly to head height.

His violet eyes glowed brighter. The ball glowed

too, the same intense violet.

Charlie moved a hand in a horizontal circular motion and the ball started to rotate.

There was silence except for a faint hum from the ball which, by now, was spinning at a very fast rate.

Picking up a smaller ball, Charlie tossed it toward the large one in the air. Instead of hitting the large ball, the smaller one just went into orbit around it.

The crowd couldn't believe what they were seeing.

Another small ball was thrown into orbit and then another and another.

Jaws dropped.

With both arms, Charlie made a turning motion and the virtual solar system turned upside down and stayed there spinning.

Magneto hunkered in the shadows manipulating the remote control joysticks.

A drum roll built-up to a crescendo.

Charlie clapped his hands together and the balls, one by one, exploded into showers of violet sparks – and were gone.

The cymbal crashed.

The audience rose as one to a standing ovation.

Magneto raised his hand to the bowing Charlie as the clapping and whistling continued.

They trotted off into the shadows and Theo stepped into the spotlight.

"Ladies and Gentlemen, Professor Magneto and his Amazing Mechanical Man."

The crowed clapped even more enthusiastically.

The house lights dimmed to total blackness.

In the entrance tunnel, Vince and Dorrie waited for their introduction. Making sure that Dorrie was distracted, Vince pulled out a hip-flash and took a slug. He hid the flask under a flap of canvas.

A voice from the darkness cried, "And now, for your edification, the spectacular, the amazing, the breath-taking, the totally awesome, VINCENTIS…"

A spotlight stabbed down from the roof onto Vince, his arms outstretched.

A second spotlight illuminated Dorrie, arms arched above her head in a ballet dancer pose.

The spotlights followed them as they cartwheeled across the ring and clambered up onto a large safety net. They bounced a few times as if on a trampoline and climbed two metal-runged rope ladders to platforms strung between the king-poles at opposite sides of the ring.

Dorrie loosened a trapeze crossbar and launched herself out across the ring, pushing higher and higher with each swing.

Vince launched the other trapeze towards her and when the synchronisation was just right, she transferred to the other trapeze and landed~~-up~~ alongside Vince on his platform.

Vince immediately caught the trapeze and repeated the manoeuvre in the opposite direction.

They invited applause – and got it in abundance.

Dorrie pushed the trapeze out towards Vince. He

swung a few times to build-up momentum and let go of his crossbar performing a spin in mid-air before grabbing the vacant one. On the return swing, he managed two complete turns and ended up back on the opposite platform.

For their next trick, Vince and Dorrie hung upside down from their trapeze crossbars with their feet entwined in the ropes at either side. They swung towards each other. Their hands met and Dorrie released her feet, grabbing Vince's wrists tightly. She held on until the trapezes had completed their swings and twisted upwards to get her feet round the ropes again.

The tricks became progressively more difficult, with the crowd gasping and applauding each one enthusiastically.

A voice came over the speaker system, "Now, Ladies and Gentlemen, The Vincentis will perform their tour de force – a triple somersault. Can I ask you to be very, very quiet and not to use any photographic flash equipment? This is an extremely dangerous routine."

The drum rolled, quietly at first, building up gradually.

Vince was hanging upside down from his trapeze and Dorrie was standing on hers, building up momentum until she was swinging well above horizontal. At just the right moment, she released, drew her body up into a ball and spun head over heels three times. She reached out to grab Vince's arm. Fingers of one hand connected for a moment but she flew right past him. The slight touch that she did get only served to twist her course – out over the edge of the safety net.

Gasps and screams sounded from the audience as Dorrie arched towards the hard floor, her mouth wide open. Her life flashed before her – all those times she had fallen into the net when she was a twelve-year old novice. The love and trust she had with Vince before he took to drinking. Was this it? Was it all over?

Dorrie hit something soft. It felt like the safety net but she knew that she was well below and to the side of where it should be.

Looking down she saw that she was eighteen inches above the grass and sawdust of the circus ring – floating in mid-air!

A huge gasp came from the crowd.

From the edge of the ring, Charlie stepped into the spotlight, his arms wide apart and eyes glowing fiercely. With his arms moving slowly downwards, he motioned Dorrie the last few inches to the floor. Circus people ran over and helped her to sit up. She panted and threw her head back to gain composure.

Theo and Marie came across from where they were standing and lifted her to her feet. Theo's eyes traversed the back row of the seated audience and he threw his arm into the air triumphantly.

The crowd clapped furiously.

The band stabbed a long chord.

Theo put his cape around Dorrie's shoulders and led her towards the exit tunnel. They turned to the audience, raised their arms, bowed and walked off.

The Grand Finale would have been a dead giveaway had the acts been introduced one by one. With their doubling and tripling-up of personnel, it just wasn't possible for some acts to be in the ring at the same time. Instead, the ring was filled with as many people and animals as could be mustered, all parading in a circle to a raucous circus march.

Polly led her ponies, the clowns were piled into their jalopy and honking the horn. Tracy's troupe of performing dogs walked round on their back legs and her monkey sat on her shoulder clinging on in bemusement. Jeff juggled with a couple of chain-saws – not switched-on this time. Vince held Dorrie's hand high in the air and they all waved and bowed as the crowd showed their gratitude.

Theo cracked his whip one last time and thanked the audience profusely. He asked them to tell all their friends about the wonderful Roget's Circus and reminded them to visit the extraordinary sideshow on the way out.

The house lights came up as the audience filed out chatting furiously and gyrating their arms.

Was Dorrie's fall from the trapeze and subsequent saving by Charlie all part of the act? They didn't know. They didn't care. They had enjoyed themselves immensely.

Vince climbed into his trailer where Marie and Polly were comforting Dorrie. She was ashen-faced, sitting with her head cupped in her hands.

"I'm so sorry Dorrie," he said, "I…"

Dorrie look away from him and stared at the floor.

"I'm sorry sweetie," he said putting his arms around her neck.

"You freakin' near killed me out there, asshole," Dorrie snarled back.

"Exactly what happened?" asked Polly. "I didn't see."

"The amazing Vince here was too god-damned drunk to catch me, that's what," exclaimed Dorrie.

"I wasn't drunk," bellowed Vince. "I only had a little nip to steady my nerves."

Marie shook her head.

"You gotta have a clear head for what you're doing, my boy."

Vince squeezed Dorrie tightly.

"I wouldn't hurt you for anything. You know that. You are all the world to me," he sobbed.

Dorrie look at him grimly.

"Vince, I want you to swear to me that you will never touch another drop of that stuff – not while we are working together anyway. Winter camp, that's something else."

Vince looked around and took Dorrie's hands.

"I swear," he said, holding up one hand. "I swear. I have, from this moment, just gone teetotal!"

Dorrie sobbed.

"I don't even know what happened out there," she wept. "I was falling through the air. I thought I was going to die and something ... something stopped me. What the heck was it? I just don't get it."

Marie coughed.

"Charlie. It was Charlie ... no, Magneto, that saved you. I have no idea how he did it. Hell, I don't know how he does any of that stuff. He totally freaks me out!"

There was silence for a minute.

Dorrie stood up purposefully and headed toward the door.

"Where are you going?" asked Vince.

Dorrie look back at him. "I think that some thanks are in order here. Don't you?"

Polly took Dorrie's arm and they headed over to Magneto's trailer.

It was getting dark outside. In the dim glow of distant coloured lights, Dorrie and Polly arrived at Magneto's trailer door. The door was closed and the steps folded-up. They could see a soft blue glow coming from inside.

Dorrie tapped on the door and waited.

...And waited.

She looked over at Polly with uncertainty and Polly gestured that she should try again.

Dorrie knocked harder.

Still nothing.

"Maybe he's asleep," suggested Polly.

"I'll try the window," said Dorrie, but the window was too high off the ground for her to reach. She looked round and saw a metal oil drum outside another trailer. She carried it over and placed it on the grass below the window. Polly helped her up onto the oil drum and held onto her as she craned to see through the crack below the blind. She was just about to tap the window when she saw two figures standing and facing one another in the pale light – Magneto and Charlie.

It was Charlie that moved.

He tilted his head forward and brought his hands up to hold each side of his head. He gave it a twist and lifted it up. There was another head inside.

Dorrie startled and the oil drum started to rock. Polly steadied her.

Charlie lifted his hands to Magneto's chest and opened his shirt.

Dorrie's mouth gawped.

A small panel opened in Magneto's chest and Charlie pulled out a rack of circuit boards connected by transparent tubes of blue glowing liquid.

Dorrie gulped.

"What's happening?" asked Polly.

Dorrie motioned her to keep quiet.

Charlie placed the rack on a small workbench and switched on a work light. He bent the head of the lamp a little higher and it illuminated his face.

It wasn't human!

Dorrie screamed in terror and fell off the oil can.

Polly helped Dorrie back to her feet. She was
breathing heavily and shaking her finger at the trailer,
totally unable to speak.

Brian came running up.

"What's going on?" he called.

Dorrie was shaking her head in disbelief.

A face appeared at the window. Grotesque.
Horrific.

Polly started to shake uncontrollably. Dorrie was
staring blankly into the distance in a state of utter
shock.

"Hey, you guys, chill out," Brian shouted. "It's
just Magneto doing his creepy stuff. It's all a trick. An
illusion. That's what he does. There's no such thing as
magic. It's all in your mind."

A headless chicken ran past. A poodle did a pas
de deux. Four white ponies with ostrich feather
headdresses did a passable can-can. The air filled
with a high electrostatic charge that made sparks arc
across the tips of the king-poles.

Brian pushed Dorrie and Polly flat against the
ground.

A high-pitched whine built-up from the trailer
and a bright violet light pulsed from underneath. The
four wheels folded up inside the base of the trailer
and left it floating impossibly above the ground.
The skin of the silver trailer rippled and flickered
with energy. Rivets smoothed out and disappeared.
The windows shrunk to nothing. The door blended

seamlessly into the side. The trailer morphed from its regular shape into something much more sleek. It rose slowly into the air.

With a loud whump, the vehicle shot high into the night sky in a steep arc.

It paused briefly somewhere above the moonlit clouds and winked out of existence.

Brian sat up scratching his head. He looked at the two girls and frowned.

"Well, there goes Professor Magneto. Pity."

The girls were still staring into the heavens.

"Come on, you two, the show must go on!"

# The Last Sunset

The scaly behemoth rose on its hind legs and roared defiance, flashing row after row of sickeningly terrible, pointed teeth.

The auditorium shrieked.

The image melted.

The screen went blank.

Whistles and catcalls filled the cinema.

Through the projection loops at the back, a hideous jelly-like blob oozed out into the back aisle.

Again the audience screamed, this time a different scream.

Fleeing people crashed through into the street in wild panic.


A mighty, metallic fist crashed down on the video machine.

"So this is the trash the Earth creatures call entertainment," came a voice as the television set, and the wall behind, were blasted out of existence.

Around the two troops lay a scene of carnage and devastation. Had they any human sensibility, they would have been very satisfied.

A soft whine heralded the approach of another.

"No more signs of life forms," it brayed in a monotone. "Back to the lander."

Three silhouettes glided across a gnarled landscape. Smoke billowed from the shattered buildings. Vehicles lay pulverised and inverted in the street like so many dead insects.

In the background was a tumult of shouting and yelling.

Ethel poured the boiling water over the egg in the saucepan and turned the gas up higher. The rest of the kettle's contents were emptied over a tea bag in an old, chipped mug.

"Red sky at night is a shepherd's delight," she half sang, putting the tin tea-caddy back in the cupboard.

She flicked a little switch on her hearing aid with gnarled fingers, and another switch on the radio.

The loud static startled her.

She twiddled with the tuning knob for a few seconds and turned the radio off in disgust.

The old mahogany and brass clock on the mantlepiece chimed four times. It was getting dark outside. Ethel reached for the light switch.

Nothing happened.

"Don't tell me the bulb has gone too," she thought, going into the dark hallway. The hall light was equally useless.

"Oh bother. It must be a power cut. What a nuisance."

Ethel groped her way into the front room. She passed a sofa with neat, embroidered cushions and antimacassars placed over the back and a glass-fronted cabinet stacked high with flowery china. The prints hanging on the wall had faded to blue and magenta.

She eased back the drab net curtains. There were no lights in the street, nor from the terrace of little houses across the way.

The sky had a rich red glow. She could just see a

cross-hatching of wispy aeroplane trails, catching the
last of the afternoon sun, but could not hear the din...

"Down periscope." ordered Captain Lamont.

A silver cylinder retracted back through the
broken ice.

"Get ready to take her down – as deep as she
goes."

"It doesn't look good." He glanced sideways to
the helmsman. "It looks like we are on our own!"

"There's nothing more on any frequency,
Captain," called the radio officer. "Just static..."

The captain looked round at his companions on
the control room.

"As far as we know, there isn't another naval
vessel left on the planet, there is just no defence.
We can stay down here for four months and hope
that they don't spot us, but we have to come up
sometime."

"Maybe they'll be gone by then..." said the radio
officer, more as a question than a statement of fact.

"Who knows," replied Lamont. "Will there be
anything to go back to?"

"Send a last positional code to HQ," he said to the
radio officer. "If there is a HQ..."

From a speck somewhere high above the North
Pole, a narrow beam of light stabbed down at the
submarine and a white mushroom blossomed in the
wilderness.

From somewhere else came the sound of

loud jeering...

　　🐱 🐱 🐱

Ethel pulled on her blue knitted bobble hat and checked that she had her purse.

"The Minimart will have some candles," she muttered to herself. "I hope they haven't closed yet."

She opened the front door and stepped out into the shadows.

As she crossed the empty street, she noticed that this was no ordinary sunset.

Using her right hand to steady herself against the wall, she edged along the street towards the main road.

*It's never as quiet as this on a Friday evening,* she thought. *The main road is usually choc-a-block at this time.*

Ethel reached the end of the road and turned the corner. She looked at where she expected to see the stall of neatly arranged fruit and vegetables. Her face dropped.

She stood and stared.

A bright white hole appeared in the middle of Ethel's face and grew outwards, consuming her whole head – and the street behind it...

Whistles and catcalls filled the cinema...

# Incident on Enceladus

For decades, the Universal Robotics Inc. assembly line produced robots that were one-hundred-percent perfect. No other corporation could boast such an incredibly low failure rate and high satisfaction level. It was for this reason the UR robots were leaders in their field. They supplied governments, armies and police forces where reliability and dependability were paramount.

The assembly line was fully automated and computer-controlled down to microscopic detail. The raw materials came into the factory at one end and the crated product left at the other, to be shipped-off all around the World, and beyond.

The snaking conveyer belts carried limbs, bodies and heads from the various component workshops around the periphery. In the middle of the floor, in air-filtered clean-room conditions, pneumatic arms lifted the parts and put them together. The completed shells were then taken on conveyors to the 'personality suite' where the memory chips were flashed according to customers' requirements. Regularly, the factory would stop for a few minutes while the soldering fumes and oil vapours was extracted and replaced with freshly filtered air.

Such was the precision of the manufacturing process that it was extremely rare for the quality control department to reject a shell for recycling. On the rare occasion that there was a fault after personality insertion, it was only necessary to remove the EPROM and flash a replacement. On ever more isolated occasions, a motor controller amplifier might need to be replaced. Not much else went wrong.

On the whole, UR robots leaving the factory were perfect in every sense.

Despite the high degree of automation, government rules insisted that the plant be inspected by a human every day. It was unheard of for this inspection to be anything but a formality. The man, wearing a protective helmet with his own air supply and dressed in a disposable white-coverall, would walk round the entire floor with a camera mounted on his helmet. The camera footage could be used as evidence should any fault in the line be missed. A line-stoppage was very expensive for Universal Robots Inc. and the inspector was fully responsible. The fact that nothing ever went wrong added to the possibility that something might be missed.

Al McGovern was doing his inspection round just like he had done hundreds of times before. He worked on a rota with two other inspectors. He had never ever had to report an anomaly. Everything just worked with consummate efficiency. It was not difficult to become a little complacent in this occupation, even with the helmet-cam recording every nook and cranny.

The fault had actually started in a component workshop. By all accounts, it was a very minor excess of flashing from a rear skull casing mould. This would normally be trimmed-off and the site polished. Somehow, the excess flashing had managed to slip though. It made very little difference to the finished product - it was cosmetic at best. Had the thin titanium protrusion on the skull part stayed in place, there would have been no problem. Unfortunately, the way the skulls are assembled meant that the sliver was dislodged and hanging half-in and half-out of the scull joint. Fortunately, the robot's brain was not inside the skull, but in the chest cavity. The head only contained optical sensors and an antenna.

Al's job was to inspect the machinery that assembled the robots, not the robots themselves. That was a job for the QC department. He didn't notice the sharp sliver of metal sticking out of the skull. Why should he?

The fully programmed robot was transported to the testing area which was the second-to-last department before dispatch. It was put through its paces and every movement monitored with absolute precision. It passed all the tests, had the inspection stickers attached to its body, and it walked through to dispatch itself. Its batteries received a final charge for delivery and it stepped into a perfectly fitting shipping crate. Other machines sealed the crate, turned it horizontal, put magna-code labels on it and deposited it on a conveyor headed for the dispatch loading bay. In its shutdown mode, the robot was only using the little energy necessary to keep its wake-up circuitry working. It could maintain its sleeping state for years.

As the crate left the dispatch bay, the codes on its exterior instructed the conveyor to take it to a levi-train and then onto the spaceport, a distance of some one hundred and twenty kilometres. Eventually, it found its way into a ship headed for the moons of Saturn. It had drop-off to make at Titan, Enceladus, Mimas and Tethys. The crate was addressed to a research team on the ice world of Enceladus.

The two-year trip went smoothly. The ship was unmanned and delivered its packages from orbit using a lander. The lander unceremoniously ejected four packages onto the moon's surface and promptly returned to the orbiting ship. There was nobody there to stop for a moment to marvel at the grandeur and spectacle of Saturn's rings, spreading fully across the moon's sky.

A radio signal alerted the recipients to where the packages could be collected and a receipt given marked, 'uninspected'. Shortly after that, a small tracked vehicle collected the crates from the icy surface and took them deep into a cave on a hillside.

"The new robots have just arrived," was the message on Dr Emma Steinberg's screen.

"Ah," she thought, "about time too."

It had been almost three years since she had put in the requisition with the full specifications of the work-bots she wanted. Her old ones were not standing up to the environment as well as expected. Working on Enceladus was even more difficult for humans. It was extremely cold, with a surface temperature of -198°C. A thick sheet of ice sits on top of an underground salty liquid ocean. Emma and her crew of scientists were tasked with drilling down into this ocean in the hope of finding some form of microbial life. Thirty kilometres is a long way down.

The construction bots had finished their work of building an underground base. A labyrinth of tunnels had been cut out of the frozen ground giving them laboratories, workshops, living quarters, storage facilities and everything else they would need for an extended stay.

The drilling head was two kilometres south, accessed by a driverless train. Humans didn't need to go down there; it was too dangerous. A series of airlocks sealed the tunnel at various points along the way and were only opened for brief periods to allow the train to pass.

Progress on the drilling was on schedule and the screen on Emma's wall showed a diagram of how far they still had to go. The rotating laser drilling head turned the ice into steam, which was vented upwards into space aided by heavy duty fans. The walls were left glass-smooth as they rapidly refroze behind the searing heat.

Due to the extreme environment, much of the grunt work at the base was carried out by robots. When they arrived from Earth in their basic form, they were modified with appropriate tools and a heating system to keep them from freezing up. Their light hydraulic and lubrication oil would be useless at these very low temperatures were it not for the heat. Luckily, Enceladus has an abundance of easily obtainable methane that could be burned to produce electricity.

Emma pulled back the lid of the first crate and removed the protective foil film.

"Wonderful!" she exclaimed. "Isn't it a beauty. It's great to have shiny new models to replace the old bangers we have been stuck with until now."

She called over an assistant.

"Henri, can you get these down to cybernetics for a once over before they start doing the mods?"

Henri Durand opened a panel on the first robot's chest and activated the boot sequence. A diagnostic screen showed that all was well. The robot twitched its servos violently, recalibrated, and stood to attention. The other three units followed in order.

Dr Emma Steinberg had gained her doctorate in theoretical physics some fifteen years ago. Enceladus was only her second posting off-world. Her initial apprehension was tempered by the sheer excitement of the project and she threw herself into the work-to the virtual exclusion of any private life. Unfortunately, she expected the same from her twelve-person human team. Being coped-up on a distant and lonely moon of Saturn was beginning to take its toll.

Emma strolled into the cybernetics workshop.

"All good?" she asked.

"Yes, I'm very impressed," said Olaf Petersen, head of engineering.

"I've been thinking," said Emma, "we can't keep referring to them by their serial numbers. Can't we come up with some good names for them. There are four of them. What comes in fours?"

Henri held his hand up, "The Three Musketeers."

Emma did a double take and then nodded her head.

"Athos, Porthos, Aramis and D'Artagnan. Very good, but they are all men. Seems a bit unfair. There should be a couple of ladies."

They pondered for a minute.

"I've got it,' said Olaf, "How about Mickey, Minnie, Donald and Daisy?"

The all laughed.

"I like it," said Emma. "Can you put some suitable graphics on them, Olaf, but keep them clean!"

"I'm sure that I can find something in the clip-art library," he grinned.

In the space of an hour, the four robots were decorated with cartoon images. They didn't need words.

"Now," said Emma, "we need to get two of them down to the drill-head. Are their sub-personas uploaded?"

"Oh, yes," replied Olaf. "All ready to go."

"Make sure you send a couple," said Emma.

"Two, yes that's what you said before," said Olaf.

"No, I mean a couple," grinned Emma. "A male

and a female!"

"Oh, I get you," said Olaf. "Does it really matter; they are all the same?"

"It matters to me," said Emma sternly.

Olaf didn't quite know if she was being serious or not but nodded in agreement.

Mickey and Minnie were loaded onto the transit train. The journey to the drill-head would only take fifteen minutes. The tunnels were unlit and in total blackness. It didn't matter as the two robots were in standby mode and the train knew exactly where it was going.

Passing through the five airlocks, the train sped along the perfectly straight domed tunnel suspended from its monorail on the ceiling. The floor was perfectly flat, like a skating rink, and even more slippery.

When the train arrived at the drill-head, hydraulic arms lifted Mickey and Minnie down onto the ground. The floor was covered with a textured, rubberised material. Even robots couldn't walk on rock-hard, polished ice. They were brought to life and they knew instinctively what they had to do.

First thing was to connect with the rig computer. Over a wireless connection, they ran through a diagnostic routine, first for themselves and then for the drilling crown. Mickey and Minnie checked-out one hundred percent. The drilling crown was showing problems. Two of the twelve lasers were not working. Had it only been one, they would have just left it, but two down meant that the other ten would be working overtime and diminishing their lifespan risking a total failure.

The two lasers had to be replaced. There were two options: 1. Wind the crown back to the surface or 2. Go down and do it in-situ.

Mickey and Minnie connected with Olaf in the workshop. It was a decision that a human had to make. Olaf got Emma on the commlink.

"The robots have identified a problem with the lasers on the drilling crown," he explained. "Two lasers have burned-out and need to be replaced or the others might follow them."

"Mmm," muttered Emma. "The last time we had to replace lasers, we pulled the crown back up, but it was only nine kilometres down at that time. Now it is three times further."

"Yes," said Olaf, "and you remember how long that took."

"Set us back a couple of weeks," moaned Emma.

"We have another option," said Olaf. "Send a robot down to do the repairs. It could slide down the tethering cable and swap-out the faulty units."

"Is that even possible?" said Emma, with arched eyebrows.

"I don't see why not," answered Olaf. "These new robots are a lot more capable than the old ones. We would attach a safety cable so it wouldn't be in any danger and we could use that to yank it back up. The whole process can be monitored by video."

"And getting the replacement lasers down there?" asked Emma. "They are too big for the robot to carry."

"We would have to winch those down separately. It's not a problem, we have plenty of winches."

"Okay," said Emma. "Let's go for it. Do you think that the two robots can handle the job by themselves?"

"Don't forget the old models," smiled Olaf. "There are five of them on-site already managing the drilling and they have done okay until these upstarts arrived."

"Of course," said Emma. "Can you prepare a suitable software update?"

"I'm on it."

Minnie was dangling on a very long carbon-fibre cable. It was the closest thing to a spider's web imaginable. Occasionally, she would stabilise her descent with a hand on the stouter, main drilling cable. A short distance behind, a second cable carried a tray with the spare parts and tools, some floodlights and a video camera. From the operations room, a number of onlookers watched the progress on a video feed.

"How far down is Minnie?" Emma asked.

"Nearly there," said Chandra Merchant, the chief operations manager. "Another ten minutes."

"By the way, why did you send Minnie and not Mickey?" asked Emma curiously.

"Didn't really matter," shrugged Chandra. "Ladies first?"

Emma clenched her lips.

A computer monitor displayed a diagrammatic cross section of the drill-hole. A flashing red dot showed Minnie's current location.

"We had to turn the laser crown off temporarily for the operation," explained Chandra, "not only because of the heat, the stream would have blinded the robot and our video feed."

Emma nodded in understanding.

"Thatagirl," said Emma as Minnie drilled-in the last bolt. The laser's umbilical connection was already in place.

"Can we do a cold diagnostic?" asked Emma. Chandra nodded and tapped a few keys on his terminal.

"Everything looks okay."

"Okay, let's try a low power burn," ordered the doctor.

"Five-percent power," said Chandra. "Oh, hold on a minute, we had better pull Minnie and her toolbox up a bit for this, just to be safe."

The cables were wound in by twenty metres.

"That should be okay," said Chandra. "Firing up on five-percent power."

The laser crown came to life with a dull glow and started to rotate.

"I'm increasing by another five," he said, tapping a key. As soon as he did that, the exhaust fans kicked-in.

"Damn," he yelled, but it was too late. The fan blades had already cut-through the cables that held Minnie and her toolbox. The video feed went dead. Minnie fell past the laser crown, deflecting only the slightest burn with her polished titanium body shell. The toolbox didn't come off so well. The ten percent power from the laser was more than enough to melt the thin tray and its contents. It joined Minnie in the hemispherical ice face below – in total darkness.

"Power off," shouted Emma and Chandra hit the Escape key.

"Now what do we do?" demanded Emma in exasperation. "We have a very expensive robot lying beneath the drill crown. We can't pull it up and I don't want to sacrifice it to the lasers and go on drilling."

She drummed the desk with her fingers. Any option she could think of would be very costly. If they retracted the drill-crown to get at the robot underneath, it would set them back months of work. If they resumed working the robot would be vaporised by the powerful lasers.

"Could we lower the drill crown gently so that Minnie could haul herself up on top and then send down another cable with a harness?" asked Emma.

"Trouble with that idea," said Chandra, "is that we could crush the robot or damage the crown, or both. We can't see what we are doing and this thing," he tapped the computer screen, "isn't accurate enough.

"Can we contact Minnie?" asked Emma.

She stabbed a button on the commlink.

"Olaf, are you getting anything from Minnie?"

"No," said the Norwegian. "Out of range. Mickey is responding."

"Can't we use Mickey as a relay?" asked Chandra from behind Emma.

"Perhaps, let me try," replied Olaf. He keyed-in a series of commands.

"I'm getting back some diagnostics," he shouted. "There is no visual but she seems to be functional."

"There is no visual because there is no light," suggested Emma.

"Quite."

"Can we power-up the lasers a fraction to provide some illumination?" asked Emma.

"Too risky," said Chandra. "Sledgehammer to crack a nut."

"What can we do?" asked Emma.

There was no reply.

Lying in the four-metre dish at the bottom of the drilling well, Minnie was in a quandary. Robots don't feel fear or even anxiety but she was applying logic to her situation. She did her best to stand upright. It was not easy on the slippery ice but she was at the bottom of a hemispherical depression which made it slightly less difficult.

Then, something happened.

A slight spark blinked inside her head.

A sliver of titanium flashing, dislodged by her tumble, had fallen across two pins of an interface chip in her video circuitry. In the total darkness, she could suddenly see. It was a very noisy vision due to the extreme amplification of her sensors. Ice is not solid rock. Even at thirty metres down, some light gets through – just the faintest glow – but it was enough for Minnie to see the laser crown hanging above her head.

She sent a signal to Mickey and Mickey passed it on to Olaf.

"Look," yelled Olaf. "I'm getting visual from Minnie. It's almost lost in noise but I can see the outline of the drill crown."

"Measure distance to drill crown," he sent to Minnie.

Minnie triangulated the distance as best she could with her binocular vision.

<5.82 metres> came the reply.

"Chandra, can you lower the crown by three metres?" he asked.

"Are you sure?" asked Chandra.

"Yes, bear with me," said Olaf.

A loud metallic reverberation filled the drill-hole as the crown was lowered.

"Measure distance to drill crown," Olaf instructed Minnie.

<2.75 metres>

"Can you touch it?" asked Olaf.

<Negative. 650 millimetres short.>

"Chandra, can you take the crown down another

half metre?" asked Olaf. By this time, Emma was at his side and watching intently.

"No, I don't have that that degree of control," came the answer. "Not from here."

"Could Mickey do it?" asked Emma.

"Possibly," replied Chandra. "If he was to mark the main cable and operate the winch from the drill head console, he could inch it down while watching the mark on the cable."

"Great, let's try it," said Emma.

"On your head be it," smiled Chandra.

"As long as it's not on Minnie's head, I'll be happy enough," she snapped back.

When the drill crown was within arm's reach, Minnie grabbed hold of a blast shield and hauled herself up. She squeezed through the gap between the laser heads and the perfectly cylindrical shaft wall and made her way to the top side of the crown. She grabbed hold of the main cable and balanced perfectly.

"Harness on its way down," called Chandra, but it was more for the benefit of the rest of the team than for Minnie. When it reached her, she strapped it on and waited patiently for the long trip to the surface.

The video feed in the drill-head chamber showed Mickey reach out and help Minnie onto the non-slip surface. They both stood motionless.

Emma wiped her brow with a tissue.

"Oh my, I'm glad that I don't have to go through

that every day. Look at Mickey and Minnie standing there like a couple of statutes."

She pointed at the image on the screen.

"You would think that, at least, she would give him a hug."

When Emma entered the cybernetics lab, Minnie was lying wide open on a workbench. Olaf was examining the robot's innards with a torch and series of data probes.

"I don't understand it," said Olaf. "Down there, she should not have been able to see anything but she was able to send back an image of sorts. I wouldn't have thought that possible."

He removed the screws that held the head shell together and pulled the two halves ajar. Inside the front half were two servo-driven cameras and a few ribbon cables connected to the main processing board. He disconnected the cables that went down through the neck to the chest and another connector joined to a power supply regulator in the top of the cranium. The back half of the skull came away freely in his hand. He laid it down carefully on a tray on his bench.

He turned over the populated front head-shell. Something small fell out onto the bench.

"What's this?" he said, picking it up with a pair of forceps. He switched-on his magnify lamp and held the small object in the light.

He showed it to Emma.

"I'm not sure what it is or how it got in there," said Olaf. "Looks like a flake of titanium. Must have got in there during manufacturing. This shouldn't happen. Universal Robotics have been sloppy. I'm going to complain about this. This is just ridiculous."

Emma shook her head slowly.

"I don't think so, Olaf. If it wasn't for this 'sloppiness', we might not still have our robot. Chill out, man!"

# The Quantum Quill

When Jane Cholmeley-Smythe was asked at her swanky dinner parties what she did for a living, she would always answer, "Oh, I write," looking down her nose at the questioner.

This was true. She did write.

When the following question would inevitably come, "I wonder if I have read any of your books?", Jane would suddenly spot an old friend on the other side of the room.

The truth was, Jane had never had a book published in her life.

'Dear Ms. Cholmeley-Smythe, having reviewed your manuscript, 'A Regency Romance', we do not feel that it is right for us at this time.'

The reject slips piled-up in her mahogany desk drawer.

Fortunately, Jane was not dependent on royalties from books: her late husband, Cecil, had left her very comfortably catered for. When she was not trying to write (she could barely put a sentence together, never mind a book), she lounged in the nineteenth-hole at the golf club or attended posh dinner parties.

Her bank account allowed her to be posh. Her early life was another story. Had Cecil Cholmeley-Smythe not become infatuated with the young barmaid and done 'the decent thing' when she became pregnant, her life would have been very different.

Amongst the reject slips in the morning mail was a

junk mail envelope. She had almost thrown it into the wastepaper basket when she noticed the red lettering above her name and address, 'Write like a Pro. Open Now!'

She opened the envelope with her silver paper knife and took out the contents.

'You too can write like a pro. The Quantum Quill is a highly advanced word processor. Even if you can't put two words together, our state-of-the-art quantum computer's artificial intelligence can construct your masterpiece in minutes. Join the ranks of the literary greats now at the press of a button!'

Following that was just a web address, no other contact details. Jane was sceptical, but she went to the web page anyway. It transpired that The Quantum Quill was not a software product that she could buy and load onto her ancient PC – it was an online service. She had to subscribe to it, and it wasn't cheap. All the AI work was done by some massive server somewhere in The Cloud. Jane had heard of The Cloud, but hadn't an inkling about its nature. She read-on.

'Simply choose the time period for your novel, the number of words you would like it to have and enter as many keywords as you wish. Press the 'Submit' button and have a cup of tea. Your masterpiece will be emailed to you in your chosen file format.'

The idea sounded absolutely intriguing. Jane signed-up immediately, giving her credit card details and return email address.

Having access to the subscribers' area of the web site, Jane could see that the process was not as 'instant' as the blurb suggested. There was a form, some ten pages long, that she had to fill-in. It wanted to know just about every aspect of the characterisation, plot, sub-plots, notable events in the historic period, and what the main protagonist's food preferences were. She felt conned. This was all much too complicated.

Annoyed and frustrated, she clicked on the FAQs button. Maybe that would tell her how to circumvent some of this drudgery. Surprisingly, it did.

'If you would like to access the Quantum Quill premium service to simplify your submission, you can upgrade here.'

It went on to explain how The Quantum Quill had access to the sum total of the knowledge of the human race and could draw from history, literature and … the science and geography aspects were of little interest to her.

Jane paid the extortionate extra fee. The ten-page submission form was whittled down to one. This was more like what the blurb had promised. They had neglected to mention the 'extras' from the outset.

Never mind. To be able to author a piece of classic literature, guaranteed, was well worth the price. She started to fill in the form, mostly from pop-up menu choices.

```
Novel type: Historical Romance
Length: 100,000+ words
Style: Classic
Period: Early 1800s
Main protagonist: Male
Occupation: Sea captain
```

The keyword text box allowed her to enter a few keywords or phrases separated by commas. She entered…

'Handsome, craggy sea captain, tempestuous relationship, obsession, vengeance, shipwreck…'

"There, that should make it interesting." She smiled inwardly.

Submit.

'Thank you for your submission. Your finished manuscript will be forwarded to the email address you supplied for your profile. Please allow up to one hour at busy times for receipt.'

One hour! She was only one hour away from literary fame. The fortune was less important.

Jane made a cup of tea and waited by her computer for the 'ting' of an incoming mail.

She wondered how this artificially intelligence would plumb the sum total of man's knowledge and come up with a literary classic. How many more could she produce in the coming months with her subscription?

She waited.

It was just under the hour with much hopeful expectation that the mail finally arrived in her inbox. She opened it with excitement. The 'book' was sent in a zip file that she had to expand. It seemed to take forever. The enclosure had a cryptic numerical filename.

'JCS10147-26062023'

She clicked on it. The words finally appeared on her screen in all their glory.

"Oh, this is excellent," she smiled, reading out the first few words aloud.

"Call me Ishmael…"

# The Hounds of Xunia

A small, silver moon-hopper lowered itself down
onto the rocky world of Xunia on three plumes of gas.
The disturbed moon-dust had barely settled when
a hatch opened and three strange craft emerged,
hovering.

Vahuxa rippled her peripheral tendrils against the
edges of the circular cloud scooter and settled gently
to the ground. She had seen the tracks of the fearsome
grunth from above and was determined to catch it.

"Have you seen the tracks, Tuvoo?" she thought
to her sister.

"Oh, yes. They are very clear. We will have it."

"I will have it," said Vahuxa emphatically.

"We will see," said Tuvoo.

The second cloud scooter glided onto the surface
of the craggy moon. 'Cloud scooter' was somewhat of
a misnomer. It could not scoot amongst the clouds; it
could fly barely two spans off the ground. The name
came from its appearance. It looked like a cloud as it
was surrounded by a very light gas halo that kept it
aloft. The rider stood on it and controlled it with an
implant.

"Where are the seeker-hounds," asked Vahuxa.

"Right behind me," replied Tuvoo.

Another cloud scooter drifted silently to the
ground. As it touched the surface, a number of
irregular-shaped black objects spilled-off. Each one
levitated off the ground on two sets of electrostatic
tripods, one on either side. They sat motionless,
waiting for an order.

The moon's surface was bathed in the light

from the hunters' home planet, Psethion, which dominated the black sky. The hilly surroundings were punctuated by long, dark shadows.

The two piloted cloud-hoppers sped past sharp, angular rocks into a small clearing followed by the empty one.

"Grunth!" shouted Vahuxa, pointing. Immediately the black shapes glided into the landscape, spinning their nebulous blue tripod legs at a rapid pace.

"Let's see how the vermin deals with a seeker," sneered Tuvoo. Her low conical shape rocked backwards and forwards on her peripheral tendrils as her biosensors probed the dark world.

"Remember, this one is mine," said Vahuxa. "Keep off!"

"It's not yours," snapped Tuvoo. "It's whoever catches it."

Vahuxa was amused. Here was her little sister, a novice grunth hunter, telling her the rules.

"If it doesn't get you first, sister!" she laughed. Indeed, many inexperienced hunters underestimated the prowess of the creature and didn't live to tell the tale.

"Wait, the seekers have a trail already," said Tuvoo. "They will soon flush it out."

A grunth was long and flat with 768 short legs and a powerful set of venomous mandibles at the front of its head. Its scaly body provided armoured protection against physical impacts and could crush any prey that ventured close. It was also very fast! With so many legs to propel it, it could move lithely across any horizontal or vertical surface and as Vahuxa's late sister found out to her cost, it could jump surprising distances. The high value of grunth venom to the pharmaceutical industry on their home planet made these hunting trips very profitable for Vahuxa and her sisters, but it wasn't a simple matter of killing the beast and milking its mandibles. Venom from a dead grunth is useless as it congeals seconds after its death and loses all its potency. The mandibles have to be milked while the creature still lives, so it has to be stunned with a neuro-blaster, milked, and then killed. They were no use to anyone once they have been milked.

The grunth moved in a slow circle as the seekers surrounded it. It didn't quite understand what they were but sensed the danger. The seekers inched closer, emanating a series of low hisses. Fine red beams of laser light stabbed at the creature, making it increasingly angry.

The grunth lunged towards the nearest seeker, trying to grab a leg or two in its pinchers, but the insubstantial tripods offered no resistance whatsoever. It was like trying to grab a sunbeam. Frustrated and annoyed, the creature whipped its back end round and hit a seeker an almighty whack with its long tail. The seeker was knocked hard against a rocky outcrop and fell to the ground. Seconds later, its two tripods reactivated and it scurried back into the encircling body.

"That's it, my pets. Hold it there while I catch up," thought Vahuxa, as she raised her cloud scooter slightly and stood up on her three main tendrils to get a better view of the situation. "The seekers have it trapped," sent Tuvoo. "I will go round the other side."

"Be careful," thought Vahuxa back.

Traversing the surface of the rocky moon was difficult for a cloud scooter. It could not hover more than a few spans from the surface and had to circumnavigate the larger rocks.

By now, the grunth was getting very agitated by its entrapment and was lashing out at the pack of seekers with its tail. Occasionally, it would score a hit on something more solid and a seeker would ricochet off a distant rock but would fall back into place when it recovered from the blow.

"I'm going to take a shot at it," thought Tuvoo. "I am closest."

"No, I told you, it's mine," returned Vahuxa. "Don't you dare! The prize is mine."

Tuvoo raised her neuro-blaster and aimed it at the beast. She didn't even get close to taking the shot. A long whip-like tail lashed out and enveloped her body. The grunth rolled itself over, pulling Tuvoo in towards her. It pulled back its monstrous head ready to strike a fatal blow.

Zap!

The shot from Vahuxa's neuro-blaster hit it squarely on the head. It squirmed, slumped, and lay still.

Vahuxa jumped off her scooter and went over to the coil of tail that was wrapped around Tuvoo's shell. She wasn't moving. Vahuxa used her long tendrils to unwrap the limp tail.

"Tuvoo, are you alright?"

A half stunned Tuvoo sent, "I'll be alright, sister. Give me a moment."

When Tuvoo was mobile again, the seekers were called up close and ordered to stand by. Each seeker had a neuro-blaster that was more precise than the hunters'. Their electronic brains reacted much faster too.

Vahuxa retrieved a clear flask from her scooter. She undid the top seal and moved towards the front of the grunth. She lifted its head and forced the mandibles down hard against the edge of the flask. A flow of yellowish liquid began to fill the vessel.

"Come on my beauty," she thought. "Give it to me. It is all mine; I won't share it with Tuvoo. She was too stupid."

As the last drop of venom dripped into the flask, Vahuxa knew that her job was done. She carefully sealed the lid and put the flask into a protective pouch.

Tuvoo was annoyed.

"Aren't you going to share the venom with me? I did help you."

Vahuxa focused her thoughts towards Tuvoo.

"No. You were foolish. You went too close to the grunth and I had to save you. You owe me your life, is that not payment enough?

Tuvoo sighed.

"Indeed, thank you my dear sister. I was a fool. I will never be a hunter such as you."

Vahuxa commanded the seekers onto their cloud scooter. Tuvoo was already standing on hers.

"Must get this flask back to the emptor," she sent, "it should be worth a good sum."

"Why such a hurry?" sent Tuvoo. "We have time to catch another grunth. One for me?"

Vahuxa mounted her scooter, turned a dial on her neuro-blaster, and shot the still-stunned grunth. It writhed for a second and split open. Its innards spilled out onto the ground.

"Ugg!" sent Tuvoo. "Did you have to do that?"

"Yes," sent Vahuxa. "It may have been milked of its venom but it is still lethal. It would be very angry if it wakes and finds us nearby. No, I want to get back and claim my bounty."

The three cloud scooters headed back towards the moon-hopper. As they rounded an outcrop of rock, Vahuxa and Tuvoo both saw a long shape arc through the sky from a ledge above. It smashed into Vahuxa's scooter and knocked her flying to the ground. Vahuxa was lying on her side, her vulnerable underside totally exposed. She struggled hard to get back to an upright position but the grunth was already bearing down on her, its mandibles snapping furiously. Such was the ferocity; it must surely have been the mate of the one she had just killed looking for vengeance. It was easily twice the size, must have been a female.

Tuvoo levelled her blaster. She was shaking wildly. The shot missed the creature by a span. She fired again. The second shot was closer but still did not hit the monster. It backed off. Tuvoo reactivated the seekers and knocked into their scooter. The five hounds tumbled onto the ground and were instantly elevated to their working positions on their twin tripods.

"Grunth," she barked at them. "Seek!"

The five seekers surrounded the grunth and stabbed at it with lasers. It writhed in pain angrily.

Tuvoo steered over to where Vahuxa was still struggling and helped her back into a stable position. The grunth lashed-out at the seekers with its rear end. One of them was sent crashing against a rock face. This one did not recover. Its tripods faded and it rolled across the ground broken and lifeless. Vahuxa climbed onto her cloud-scooter. It seemed to be undamaged, but she was still in a state of shock and only just managed to get it aloft.

"I will take care of this beast," she sent.

"No, Vahuxa," replied Tuvoo. "This one is mine. You owe it to me."

"Your marksmanship is not up to it," sent Vahuxa.

"Maybe," answered Tuvoo, "but my hounds will help."

Tuvoo sent a command to the four remaining seekers. In unison, they unleashed their neuro-blasters into the creature's body. It arched in pain and fell stunned and motionless.

Tuvoo took her flask and unmounted the scooter. The grunth lay still in front of her. She pulled back its head and slammed its mandibles into the mouth of the opened flask as she had seen Vahuxa do earlier. The deadly venom spurted in.

"Ah, this will be a profitable hunt," she thought. "This is a large one, there will be much venom."

So enthralled was she with her prize, she didn't notice the creature's tail twitch. In a split second, it had whipped round and encircled her body – just as the other one had. She dropped the flask and some of it splashed across her side.

Tuvoo screamed in agony.

Vahuxa sent an order to the seekers. They fired at full power. Vahuxa would never have dared to fire full power with her neuro-blaster, not with her sister in the way, but the hounds were closer and much more accurate. The grunth stopped moving and released its grip. Tuvoo slipped out. With Tuvoo well clear, Vahuxa released an almighty blast into the grunth. It erupted in a mass of entrails.

Vahuxa could see that Tuvoo was hurt. The small splash of venom had hit her shell, which was fairly resilient, but it had also landed on some of her delicate tendrils. They were limp, withered and useless.

"Can you walk?" sent Vahuxa.

"No, I am hurt, half of my tendrils are gone."

"Oh, my poor sister. Let me help you."

"Be careful, Vahuxa. There may still be venom on my body."

Vahuxa summoned the four remaining seekers to help move Tuvoo onto her scooter.

"There, my dearest. Are you steady?"

"I'll be alright. To think that I let myself be outwitted by grunths twice this hunt. I'm very lucky to have you with me, sister."

"And I am lucky to have such a brave little sister. In time, you will match my prowess, you'll see. Maybe, surpass it."

"We had better go home," sent Tuvoo. "Too much adventure for one day."

"Haven't you forgotten something?" asked Vahuxa.

"What?"

Vahuxa held-up a flask of yellow venom. It was almost full.

"This, my sister. You are going to very rich!"

# Eternity Stone

"I bet it's worth a fortune!" exclaimed the boy.

"Maybe. Maybe. I wouldn't like to have to put a price on it," said the balding old man with the eye-glass.

"How did you come by it, Sonny?"

The youth hesitated.

"It's mine. I found it," he replied. "I found it ... on the ground!"

"Mmm."

The old man held it up to the light with a pair of tweezers and twisted back and forward with a certain fascination.

"Well, what will you give me for it," asked the boy impatiently.

"Nothing, my boy," came the reply. "I'm afraid I can't take it."

"But why not?" protested the youth. "I bet it's worth a fortune..."

Paul unfurled his handkerchief on the curator's desk.

"Mr Bernstein said it was worth a fortune," he explained.

The curator peered at it through his bifocals.

"Interesting, you say you found it in a field?" he asked.

"Yes, just up behind the Foster's place, yesterday," Paul volunteered, as the man handed it back and looked at his watch.

"Is that the time? Very interesting, I will be in touch..."

"That's five you owe me," demanded the big boy holding out his hand.

"I haven't got it," whispered Paul.

"You shouldn't play if you haven't got the stake. I think I'll just take it out of your hide," said the bully, straightening up and looking down on the wretch.

"No, wait," whimpered the youth, holding up a crumpled handkerchief and opening it out in his hand.

"It's worth a lot of money, the curator at the museum said so."

"Clear off before I knock your head in!" said the gruff voice. "Keep out of my way or you are in big trouble."

Paul snatched up his treasure and ran off down the alley.

"Ryan!"

The science master's voice made Paul jump.

"What are you playing with, bring it up here at once."

Paul edged up to the front of the classroom and put the object on the desk.

"I've told you before Ryan, you are not to bring your distractions into the class. What is this?"

"Don't know Sir."

The master rolled it around the top of his dark stained desk-top with his forefinger, eyeing it curiously.

"What have I just been talking about?" he said sternly.

Paul looked about blankly. He glanced down at the object on the desk top and up at the blackboard.

"Feldspar, Sir."

"What about Feldspar."

"It has two different refractive indexes, Sir."

"Indices, boy, indices!"

"Yes Sir, indices."

The master pushed the object back across the desk.

"Put this away and go back to your seat. If I see you with it again I will confiscate it. Understand?"

"Yes Sir..."

Pauls legs dangled down over the side of the little wooden jetty where he often stopped on his way home from school. Across the river, he could hear the screech of a circular saw as it ran down the length of a log of freshly cut pine in the timber yard.

He rolled the tiny object in the palm of his hand and marvelled at the way it caught the soft summer sunlight. It was greyish in tone but reflected colours that he had never seen before. It seemed to live, with a sparkle that went down much deeper than its surface could allow.

It rolled between his fingers and fell out of his hand. He gasped as it plopped into the dark water below.

Thaddeus Foster spread a gingham napkin on his lap and poured a glass of milk. Out through the window, and behind the barn, he admired the rich autumnal colours in the trees.

Maggie set a hot plate down in front of him, smiled, and headed back into the kitchen. Thaddeus loved fresh trout, especially the way Maggie cooked it.

He slit the fish lengthways with his knife and pulled on the long white bone. A small, sparkling object fell out onto to his plate. He turned it over with the tip of his knife. *What's this? A pebble? A piece of some fancy fishing lure?*

His attention was broken by a yell from the kitchen.

"Thaddeus, that big crow is back, and it's at the fruit again..."

He jumped up from the chair, dropping his napkin and fork on the floor. Taking the small object from the edge of his plate, he headed for the kitchen.

From the coat hooks by the door, he grabbed a home-made catapult and ran out into the garden. The fat bird was gorging itself on ripe berries through the netting.

Thaddeus put the small object into the leather tongue of the catapult and pulled back hard on the strong rubber. As he levelled the fork at the black scavenger, it flapped off into the air. The bird did not even notice the small missile as it whistled past, wide by a good five feet, and it was a long way off by the time the object reached the top of its trajectory and started on its curved path back towards the ground.

As it tumbled through the air, it reflected needles of light from the orange, evening sun like the mirrored ball in a dance hall. Somehow, it flickered out of existence for an instant and came back again. It hit the earth of a fallow field beyond.

A daydreaming schoolboy meandered along the stony path. On either side, primroses held their proud heads above the fresh, new grass and a butterfly fluttered erratically across his line of vision.

Paul Ryan was late for school again. He didn't care.

His grubby shoe kicked something small and shiny. He bent down and picked it up.

"Looks like a diamond or something," he said to himself.

He rolled it up in a starchy linen handkerchief that his mother had forced into his pocket earlier.

After school, Paul wandered down the main street. He stopped outside a shop and looked in the window. On display were three blue velvet stands adorned with gold necklaces and charm bracelets, each one with a tiny, indecipherable price tag.

A bell tingled at the back of the shop as he opened the heavy door.

"I bet it's worth a fortune!" exclaimed the boy.

"Maybe. Maybe. I wouldn't like to have to put a price on it," said the balding old man with the eye-glass.

"How did you come by it, Sonny?"

# Montague

"Where's the other one?" smiled the young man behind the desk.

"The other one?" asked the elderly lady. "The other what?"

The assistant pointed at the dilapidated droid standing behind her.

"I thought that they went into the ark in twos," he mused.

"Humph!" she grunted. "Young man, I will have you know that Montague has served me impeccably for twenty-five years."

"Montague?" he sniggered.

"Twenty-five years without so much as a hiccup," she continued. "My name is Wylie and I have an appointment for ten thirty."

The assistant tapped a few keys on his terminal and tried desperately to conceal his giggles.

"Yes. Mrs Wylie, and ... Montague," he said in his most professional tone. "So what seems to be the trouble?"

"Montague has not been feeling too well lately," she said, peering down her nose through a small pair of glasses. "I would like someone to have a look at him."

The assistant tried to keep a straight face. "Could you be more specific?"

"He is just not himself," she went on. "He has started tripping over things. Spilled my tea all over the bed yesterday morning."

At this stage the assistant just had to turn away as tears were running down his cheeks.

"Just a minute," he managed to get out, if somewhat garbled. "I'll just speak to the manager."

He quickly disappeared behind a screen.

"What's so funny, Collins?" asked the manager.

The young fellow wiped his eyes and pulled himself together.

"There's an old dear outside with an RBX5 ... calls it Montague ... must be fifty years old if it's a day. She says it's not feeling too good..."

The manager grinned.

"An RBX5?" he said in a deliberate tone. "I haven't seen one of those since I was a boy. You say it is actually with her?"

"Yes. It's not too steady, but it followed her in."

The manager stepped out into the reception area and gave a slight bow.

"Good morning Madam. I am George Mueller, the service manager. My, he is a fine specimen."

"Good morning," she scowled. "Would you kindly have a look at Montague. I am getting nothing but impudence from that young assistant."

Mueller shooed the young man away.

"Of course Madam." He smiled his best smile. "Take him over to bay five ... over there."

She looked where he was pointing and led the robot by the hand.

The diagnostic screen flipped through page after page of diagrams and circuit drawings. It paused every now and then, highlighting certain areas, and then spewed out a stream of hard copy. Mueller went on tapping at the keyboard and occasionally shaking his head. He put another memory cube into the laser drive and the screen filled with lists and symbols.

"I'm afraid we don't have the correct service manual for this model, Madam. I can only do some basic tests. He has seen better days you know."

She scowled again and patted the robot.

"I have had Montague since my husband George died. He has been very good to me."

The manager paused, trying to think of a way to explain.

"Madam. Montague is old, very old. His bearings are all worn out. His hydraulics have no pressure left in them. Half of his circuits have packed up."

"Well, fix him up then," she demanded.

"It's not as simple as that," came the reply. "The spare parts are not available any more, they are obsolete. I mean, this kind of gyrator went out of production twenty years ago..."

"Don't you have something that would do? Couldn't you patch him up somehow? You do come very highly recommended," she grumped.

"We would have to practically build it from scratch Madam," he explained. "It would be very costly and certainly much cheaper to buy a new one."

"I do not want a new one! I have grown very attached to Montague."

"Look Madam," he went on, "I do not normally do this, but I would be prepared to take him in part exchange for a RBX600. It's not the latest but it is a newer model. It can do all the same things, and a lot more..."

"No!" she exclaimed. "I want my Montague. I have no time for these ... these new-fangled gimmicks."

Mueller cupped his head in his hands. Outside the service bay, young Collins was nudging a white coated girl with his elbow.

"One lump or two?" he said in his best robotic voice, and mimed a trip over an invisible cat. She giggled too.

Mueller spoke-up to disguise the tomfoolery outside.

"Tell me, Madam. What duties does the droid do for you?" he asked.

"Everything," she replied. "He is my butler, my housekeeper, my cook and my chauffeur..."

"You let this thing drive?" he gasped.

"Of course, Montague's a very good driver."

The manager slapped his forehead with the palm of his hand and disconnected the diagnostic umbilical.

"I am sorry to say that I ... that Nova Cybertronics ... cannot help you Madam," he said, standing up.

She was visibly annoyed.

"Can you suggest someone else then?" she demanded.

The manager stood shaking his head and looked round as young Collins came into the room.

"You could try these people," he smirked. "They might be able to help."

He held out a piece of paper. Mueller glanced at it and put his hands over his eyes. Taking it from him, Mrs Wylie turned and put her nose in the air. "Come, Montague. Let's go..."

The sleek limousine glided through two battered doors into a yard and stopped. It was like a scene from a televid of the robotic wars. The tottering robot stepped out of the car and opened the rear door for its elderly mistress.

"Is there anybody here?" she called, weaving her way through a maze of chassis and dismembered limbs.

"Hello..."

A human face appeared over a pile of dull stainless steel and panels of scorched khaki.

"Yeah. What do you want Missus?"

"I was told that you could repair my ... android," she called back.

A scruffy man in his late forties stepped out into the open and looked her up and down with shifty eyes. He glanced over at the shining automobile and its driver who was standing to attention beside it.

"Yeah sure," he said, wiping his brow with an oily rag. "Bring it in."

"End of the week," said the mechanic, putting down his electric screwdriver.

"Humph," she grunted, "and that lot round at Nova Cybertronics told me that it was impossible, that there were no spare parts."

The mechanic winked. "Just leave it to me. That mob could fix nothing; they are only interested in selling new droids."

"Oh, how am I going to get back home now?" she whined and nodded in the direction of her driverless car.

"Mm," said the shifty-eyed one, looking around the workshop. "I could let you borrow one of these."

He slapped the back of a dormant droid. It had green camouflage markings and gaping holes where a rat's nest of multi-coloured wiring spilled out.

"It's not much to look at, but it can drive," he said quickly.

"It looks damned dangerous to me!" she exclaimed.

"Don't worry, it's not going to do anything ... now." He kicked a long ugly looking perforated metal cylinder under the work bench. "It's quite harmless, and it's only for a couple of days."

Dorothy Wylie looked into the videophone at another face-lifted female.

"Yes, Shirley, they fixed Montague up as good as new."

"Oh really," said the voice from the wall. "They were able to find the bits?"

"No problem," said the pink-haired one. "I'm so pleased. Dear old Montague, life just wouldn't be the same without him."

"Well I'll be able to see him when I come round later," said Shirley. "Chaio."

Shirley put her cup and saucer down on the coffee table with a clatter.

"Dorothy," she said slowly. "Are you sure about Montague?"

"Oh what do you mean, Darling. He's just fine."

"No. There is something peculiar about the way he looks at me. His eyes..."

"Stuff and nonsense!" insisted Dorothy. "You are imagining it. Oh dear me, the idea. Montague, pour Shirley another cup of coffee."

The robot poured the coffee into the cup and indicated the cream jug with his hand.

"Just a splash," she said, watching his every move.

"I'll be back in a minute," said Dorothy, stepping out into the hallway.

Shirley stared at the robot.

The robot stared at Shirley.

She stirred her coffee nervously.

A shriek from another part of the house sent the coffee flying into the air.

"Shirley. Shirley. Come quickly," came the voice.

On the bathmat lay the twisted form of a small white poodle.

"It's Flossie. She's dead. What could have happened to her?"

Shirley looked back at the robot that had followed her from the living room. It stood impassively.

"Oh, the poor darling," wept Dorothy, kneeling

on the floor.

"It's only half an hour ago that I asked Montague to take her for walkies."

Shirley thought for a moment. "What exactly did you say?"

"Oh I don't know," sobbed Dorothy. "What does it matter now?"

"No. It's important. Try to remember," insisted Shirley.

Dorothy pondered for a while and shook her head.

"Something like... Montague, it's time to take Flossie out. He has always done it just after she has had her lunch."

"You told Montague to take Flossie out?"

"Yes. Something like that ... Oh, I don't know," Dorothy cried.

Shirley looked round at the robot.

"Do you know anything about this?" she demanded.

The robot said nothing, but shuffled backwards. It knocked against a small fancy table supporting an ornamental vase. It wobbled.

"Montague. Look out," screamed Dorothy.

With a lunge, the robot dived across the hall, rolled over twice, and came up crouching behind a tall potted plant, an arm outstretched.

Dorothy gasped in amazement. "He ... He's never done anything like that before!"

"You really must get rid of that dreadful droid,

Dorothy," Shirley scolded from the screen on the wall.

"Shirley, Darling, he has been perfectly normal since last week," Dorothy protested. "I did try to vid the engineer to speak to him about that peculiar incident in the hall, but the channel seems to be dead."

"I'm not surprised," Shirley broke in. "Didn't you see the newscast last night?"

"What about it?"

"That place is just a hole in the ground now. They say there was an explosion. The whole area is cordoned off with radiation hazard signs."

Dorothy stared blankly at the screen.

"Oh no," she whispered, looking to the side. "I sent Montague out last night to do some tidying-up in the garage. He was gone for rather a long time."

"Ahem. Dorothy, what did you tell him to do ... exactly," asked Shirley.

"I just told him to clean out the workshop!" she replied.

Shirley eyes lit up. "I knew it," she yelled. "Don't you see? He is interpreting your innocent requests as military orders ... It's something that they have put inside him, some ex-army spares, I bet."

"Oh don't be so far-fetched Shirley, I mean ... really. Are you trying to tell me that my Montague is some sort of Jekyll and Hyde monster? Such rubbish. First you told me that he was looking at you in a funny way, now this..."

"Haven't you noticed any differences in his personality, his mannerisms," Shirley inquired patiently.

Dorothy spoke back abruptly, "No! Not at all. Apart from the fact that he seems ... younger. But that is simply because he has had an overhaul."

"It's quite easy to test my theory," Shirley insisted. "Try him with some direct military orders and watch his response."

"Alright Shirley, I will. But just to prove you are wrong..."

Dorothy wasn't very good at acting the Sergeant Major.

"'Ten shun!" she called.

The robot straightened up, but no more than he would have with any aural command from his mistress.

"Left turn."

Montague looked at her for a second and slowly spun on his left heel.

"Forward march."

He walked up to the solid living room wall, stopped and looked back inquisitively.

"I didn't tell you to stop!"

The robot pointed at the wall with its hand.

"Alright. Quick march outside to the veranda."

Montague strolled out through the French windows in his usual gentlemanly gait.

"Fall in!"

He looked down at the swimming pool and back at her with that same puzzled look. He was just about to step off the edge when she shouted.

"Stop."

The robot turned and looked at her, waiting for the next stupid order. He looked so pathetic and quite unlike any high tech commando.

He put his hands up in a kind of 'what now' gesture and knocked the pool side table and parasol into the water.

Dorothy eyed him almost pitifully and shook her head as she spoke. "Montague, you really kill me."

Shirley Grandfield peered through a black veil and watery eyes. Beside her, outside the small chapel of rest, stood Dorothy's brother.

"I tried to warn her, Edwin. But she wouldn't have it," she said blowing her nose into a lacy handkerchief.

Edwin put his arm around her and held her tightly.

"Did they ever find that droid?" he asked.

"No. It has vanished, I very much doubt if it will show its face again. I would be broken up and cast to the four winds" she muttered.

"Home, Henry," Edwin rapped at the driver. "Via Mrs Grandfield's house."

The ageing droid pulled down its visor, turned, took a long look at Shirley, and replied.

"Yes Sir. At once, Sir."

# &lt;Hiss&gt; &lt;Click&gt; Ba'tam

<Hiss> <Click> Ba'tam had what you might call an unstable personality. No, that's not totally accurate: in fact, his personality was probably the only thing stable about him. Everything else changed by the second.

Like the rest of his race, his form was in a state of constant transmutation. One minute he was as solid as a rock, the next, a nebulous green cloud. Sometimes, he would present himself as a vile brown puddle and then he would shape-shift into a gleaming metallic sphere.

Yet <Hiss> <Click> Ba'tam would continue a conversation as if nothing was happening. Except for the odd occasion when he would flip into hyperspace to perfect one of his mimicries, he was a rational as you or I. However, until you got used to him, as you can imagine, carrying on such a conversation can be quite disconcerting.

Anyway, to get to the point, it was a lovely day with Ceta's three suns casting subtly different shadows on the sandy ground. <Hiss> <Click> Ba'tam had summoned my presence in his usual arrogant way, but I understand that, after all, I can walk about, whereas he has to stay, more or less, in the same place all the time. I was never quite sure if Cetan Shapeshifters changed their shape by some conscious effort or if it was just a natural reflex, like breathing or scratching. I thought it was disrespectful to mention it but on this occasion, he was in one of his more gaseous moods – something like a frozen firework – all smoke and coloured sparks, but instead of erupting into a spectacle of starburst and whizzbangs, he just hung in the air, motionless, like a Christmas tree.

"I wonder if you could do something for me?" said <Hiss> <Click> Ba'tam, touching minds.

"But, of course," said I. "What can I do for you?"

I thought to myself, "This is strange. He's never asked me, or anyone else, to do something for him before. What could it be?"

<Hiss> <Click> Ba'tam made the mental equivalent of clearing his throat. I could just detect a certain hesitation.

"Well, you see, the problem is that I am not particularly mobile, as you are. Yes, I can drift with the winds when I'm dispersed, like this, but most of the time, I'm stuck in the same place. I would like to travel. Now, you have travelled. Travelling is good for the mind. I can sense it in you."

"Yes, I've never really thought about it but I suppose I take it for granted. Can't be much fun staying in the same place all the time?"

"You will help me then?" asked <Hiss> <Click> Ba'tam.

"Well..." I stuttered, "it's not that I'm not prepared to help you, I just don't see that it is possible, I mean..."

"Stuff and nonsense," interrupted <Hiss> <Click> Ba'tam. "Anything is possible if you put your mind to it and I've been doing that for a very long time."

"So, what's your idea?" I asked. "You keep changing form. What mode of transport do you suggest? Where do you want to go? Across the plain, the far side of the planet, Marinicia Three?"

"I would like to go to your planet. Earth."

I laughed a nervous laugh, inwardly, but he probably sensed it.

"Earth!!! But…"

"I can see the pictures in your mind," said <Hiss> <Click> Ba'tam, mentally. "Beautiful blue skies, trees, vast oceans teeming with life. I can feel your emotions; they are so rich. I want to experience those same things for myself, to share your pleasures.

The cloud that was <Hiss> <Click> Ba'tam sank to the ground and became a carpet of fog.

"But Ceta and Earth are almost identical," I said. "That's why we are here in the first place. It took hundreds of years of deep space exploration to find another planet just like Earth. Same atmosphere, same climates, same temperature range, similar gravity. Same everything except there are three suns and no humanoids."

"You tell me how similar it is, yet you still have these feelings for Earth. It must be more special," said the fog, as it lightened and floated upwards.

"What you are describing, my friend, is my homesickness. Humans always have such feeling for their place of origin."

"Sickness? Why do you call it sickness? Sickness is unpleasant yet your feelings are the very opposite. I am confused."

<Hiss> <Click> Ba'tam undissolved into a craggy purple monolith momentarily and, just as suddenly, melted to the ground like a pink blancmange.

I blinked. Here was an entity that changed its shape by the minute and it tells me that it is confused.

"Look, I don't see any way that I can take you to Earth, it would be difficult enough even getting you to the space port at Ceta City ... besides, it would cost a fortune. Who is going to pay?"

"As I have already explained," said <Hiss> <Click> Ba'tam, mentally, "I have been thinking about this for a very long time. I have a way..."

I suppose that it should have occurred to me before, but <Hiss> <Click> Ba'tam's hermetically sealed, Zero-G chamber made his erratic transformations quite irrelevant. The fact that it was stowed away in the cargo hold marked as 'radioactive mineral sample – danger!" disguised the real contents. I had better things to do on the month-long hyperspace jump than worry about the thing in the cargo hold. Getting a free trip back home was beyond my wildest dreams and I could swear that I could smell the fresh sea air when we dropped-out in Earth orbit, just level with the ecliptic.

On the few occasions that I went close enough to tele-contact my benefactor, he was still with us. He greeted me as if I had only been away for a few minutes. He obviously lived on a different timescale, or was it just that he was listening to my thoughts all the time?

There was still the problem of getting him
down to the surface. I would have to arrange for an
extra-terrestrial visa. Does such a thing exist? This
sentient life form, and his kin, had never ventured
further than their own back yard yet <Hiss> <Click>
Ba'tam seemed to have ways to get things done.
His telepathy could plunder the human mind
and discover their greatest desires. He used that
information to his own ends.

Unfair.

Immoral.

It was uncanny how he knew more about people
than they did themselves. He could probe their
deepest psyche to discover their wildest aspirations –
and remotest fears.

In a month-long hyperspace jump, one usually
meets everybody in the relatively small confines of
a jump ship. After all, it is nine-tenths engine – the
same proportions an iceberg is above and below the
water – only the tip is visible.

But, the man standing next to me at the check-in
desk was a complete stranger. He had uncommonly
good looks for a spacer. I would have put him
much more in the video star category. Yet he looked
familiar. Strangely familiar. It wasn't the flashing
smile that did it, nor the courteous 'after you', as he
walked into the narrow connecting pod. It was the
voice. The unmistakable voice-in-my-head of <Hiss>
<Click> Ba'tam.

I stopped in my tracks and looked at him.

"How…?"

"What you are seeing, dear friend, is what you want to see."

My legs went to rubber with realisation.

"Ah, I can feel that you are surprised, but this way is easier," said <Hiss> <Click> Ba'tam, with a human voice. "I don't want to be stuck in a Zero-G cargo pod for the next week while they sort out the paperwork."

"But, you don't have a passport, visa, or any identification at all. You don't officially exist!" I said. "You can't just turn-up at Earth's front door and expect nobody to notice."

<Hiss> <Click> Ba'tam's human form winked and smiled.

"As I told you, people will see what they want to see, and I think that you had better call me Barney Thomas. It's more natural, don't you think?"

Horrific possibilities crossed my mind.

"You know perfectly well what I think. That's just the trouble!"

# Entry Phone Enigma

"Shareen Gupta, I think I love you," spoke the voice from the grille on the wall.

She could hear a faint whirr as a lens rotated and zoomed in on her pretty face. She bowed her head, trying not to look embarrassed.

"Oh hurry up and open the door Melvin, I'm already five minutes late," she said.

The security camera panned down her slim figure to her shiny black shoes, and back up again, slowly.

Shareen stabbed the button beside the door deliberately. And again.

"You're so lovely," came the soft spoken voice, without the slightest hint of urgency.

"Melvin, please open the door," she pleaded pressing the button even harder.

The quiet voice spoke again.

"Shareen. I have been watching you come and go from the Transtar Tower for nearly three months now. Every morning. Every evening. And each time you step through the door, my heart starts racing ... I just had to talk to you."

Shareen twisted her mouth into a grimace and started tapping her foot on the marble doorstep.

"You wore your pink sari last Friday, didn't you?" asked Melvin.

"Yes, I was going out for the evening," she answered impatiently.

"It was most beautiful, and you were ... totally stunning."

"I'm glad you liked it. Now open the door!"

"Shareen. Would you ... ever consider ... me?"

"No! Certainly not!" she stamped.

"But, my lovely, it would make me so very happy."

"I'm beginning to lose my patience, Melvin."

The camera scanned her up and down again. It could see her long black hair tumbling over a floral patterned scarf that was neatly draped around her narrow shoulders.

"You are blushing, Shareen, aren't you?" said the voice from the loudspeaker.

"How do you know that?" she snapped.

"Infra-red, my sweetest," came the answer. "Your cheeks look bright green to me, at the moment."

"You'll be telling me next that you have X-ray eyes, I suppose!" she proclaimed sarcastically.

"Shareen, I know more about you than you can possibly imagine," came the voice, as the camera passed down her body again in a shallow arc.

"Melvin! Stop it at once, or I will report you!"

"You know, you look even more wonderful when you are angry like that," taunted Melvin.

Shareen smiled. He could see her bright, white teeth shining through the subtlest shade of lipstick. Her eyes sparkled with life in the early morning light.

"Look, Melvin. If I promise to come down to security to see you, will you let me in?" she begged.

"Yes. Oh, yes, I will," avowed Melvin. "My office is on sub-level one, just one floor down from reception."

"I know where it is," she said.

The heavy armour-plate glass door clicked and

slid open. When she stepped in, Shareen glanced back at the watching eye. As she crossed the empty marble hall, she sensed that cameras were tracking her every step.

The lift doors opened almost immediately. She went in and put out her hand to touch the button for the fourteenth floor, as she usually did, but paused. Her fingers moved down and found the button for sub-level one. The lift whined into motion.

She took a long, deep breath and stared up at the ceiling. Another lens swivelled and focused. She ignored it.

When the doors opened, Shareen looked out into an empty corridor that was only half lit with auxiliary lighting. Across the way was a door marked 'Security – Authorised Personnel Only.' She walked over to it and held her security card up to the RF reader. It opened.

Inside, the room was illuminated only by the cold light from a bank of video monitors that covered a whole wall. On the screens danced ever-changing vistas of yet empty offices. The corridors too were devoid of any activity and only a dawn delivery at a back service bay gave any clue to life.

As her eyes grew accustomed to the twilight, she looked about slowly. There were no desks or chairs. A myriad of coloured lights blinked and flickered. The soft, heavy smell of electronic circuitry filled the small room.

She got up and placed her hand gently on a black metal cabinet sitting on the floor in the corner. It felt warm to the touch and hummed a gentle song.

Looking at a video camera high up on the wall, she became aware that every monitor was showing her smiling face in a kaleidoscopic arabesque.

"Melvin," she whispered softly. "You know that this can never be..."

# Grottomatic

"Ho. Ho. Ho. Happy Christmas", beamed the white bearded face from the large video screen on the wall.

"Come right in to Lacy's Christmas Grotto and tell Santa Claus what you want for Christmas."

"Speak to him person to person with our live holophone link-up to his headquarters at the North Pole."

"Get a special gift from him through his magic transmatter machine".

A suitably festive jingle blared through the speakers accompanied by a computer animation of a long zoom-in from space to a fairy-tale castle amidst the frozen wastes of the Arctic.

Dissolving to a scene inside, an army of mechanical looking elves and dwarves assembled colourful toys with the speed and precision of a highly automated car factory. The voice droned on.

A small queue of barely interested children squiggled out into the main walkway of the mall - complete with an entourage of older brothers, sisters and adults. The adults' eyes were single-mindedly focused on the vid-screen. The kids pushed, shoved, taunted, pulled hair, fell over, threw fits and generally behaved as normal.

"Stop that, Jennifer!" screamed a young mother, pulling at her child's arm.

"If you don't behave yourself, Santa won't give you a present."

"Don't want a stupid present," grimaced the brat, "and there's no such thing as Santa Claus anyway,

Helena says so and she should know, she's seven."

The mother scowled, "Then Helena won't get any Christmas presents at all."

"Yes she will," cheeked the child, "she's getting a My-Little-Ponytron. She has found it in her mom's cupboard in the bedroom."

The door to the Grotto slid open and a four-year-old boy came out grasping a wriggling lizard-like figure.

"Look what I got mommy, ReptoMan."

The toy's gyrations were too much for the small hand and fell from its grasp. 'ReptoMan' scurried out across the mall, chased by the child and rapidly followed by a perplexed mother. They were swallowed up by the crowd.

"It's your turn, Jennifer," said the mother pulling the reluctant girl towards the grotto door.

Running a credit card through a slot with one hand, she pushed little Jennifer inside with the other. The door slid shut.

The mother ignored the hammering and kicking that was coming from the other side of the door and turned to another woman behind.

"I don't know why I bother," she sighed. "They just don't appreciate it."

"Oh, I know," said the other, "but when I was little, they had real Father Christmases, all dressed up in red and white and ringing bells. It's just not the same now, is it?"

Inside, it was dark. Very dark.

Jennifer had never really experienced total darkness before but before she had time to be frightened, a fan of shimmering red light spread across the room from one corner. Then another blue-green light washed across it from somewhere else.

Where the beams of light met, an image formed and she saw that she was inside a strange glowing cave.

The walls sparkled as if made of some kind of glass studded with myriads of tiny coloured pin-heads of light.

"Hello, Jennifer," came a voice from further back inside. "Happy Christmas."

Jennifer stepped cautiously towards the voice and could make out the shape of a small man dressed in red and sitting in a big armchair.

"You are not Santa Claus," she shouted. "I know what you are. You are just a stupid hologram."

She walked up to the image and kicked it. Her foot went straight through.

"See."

"Now, now. Jennifer. don't be like that", smiled the bearded apparition. "You are talking to me through my holophone. It's a bit like the videophone you have at home but it lets you see all of me. In the round as it were."

He laughed and rubbed his midriff.

Jennifer took a step backwards and put her hands over her ears.

"I don't believe in Santa Claus," she screamed.

"I am really here in my castle at the North Pole working hard to make presents for all the boys and girls for Christmas."

"Look."

Santa waved his hand and the room transformed into a three-dimensional version of the busy toy factory she had seen on the screen outside.

Rows and rows of robotic elves assembled toys of all kinds with unbelievable speed and dexterity.

One of the impish factory robots looked up from what it was doing and smiled.

"Hiya, Jennifer," he winked, "Nice to see you. Do you know what you would like for Christmas?"

"I don't believe in Christmas," she stamped.

"And there is NO Santa Claus. And there is NO toy factory at the North Pole."

"Oh, I see," smirked the elf, continuing with his work. "So I am just wasting my time making all these toys?"

At that, Father Christmas walked over and patted the elf on the head.

"He's a good little worker is Tyfen," he said, "but you can't waste time chatting, only a week to go you know."

"Now Jennifer, would you like to see my reindeer?"

Before she could protest, he waved his arm again and they were in an icy cold yard. Jennifer stood knee deep in snow and the wind howled around her.

"Mmm. You are not dressed for this weather young lady," said Father Christmas, putting his arm around her and whisking her through a heavy wooden door into a cosy stable. He kicked the door shut with his heel.

"Here they are. Do you know their names?"

Jennifer closed her lips tightly and folded her arms.

Father Christmas pointed at each animal in turn.

"Dasher, Dancer, Prancer, Vixen, Comet, Cupid, Donner and Blitzen."

"But what about Rudolph?" demanded Jennifer.

"Ho. Ho. Ho." laughed Santa, "There's no Rudolph. That's just a song."

"Come here Prancer, come and say hello to Jennifer."

The deer ambled over and looked down at the little girl with its big soft eyes.

It leaned down and put its cold, wet nose against her cheek. Jennifer recoiled in astonishment.

"No Prancer, you will frighten her," explained Santa Claus stroking the deer in the scraggy long hair behind its antlers.

"Now, Jennifer, what was it you wanted. It was a My-Little-Ponytron like Helena's, wasn't it?"

Jennifer, still wide-eyed, stared for a second at the reindeer, then at Santa, and nodded.

"Let me see," said Santa stroking his long white beard. He wiggled his fingers in the air and they were suddenly in a huge warehouse crammed floor to ceiling with toys.

They glided along a moving walkway that seemed to drift toward the ceiling at the same time.

"They should be around here," said Santa, running his fingers across some cartons. "Ah, yes."

He took a box from the shelf and opened it. He lifted out a small blue horse-shaped object, blew on it, and handed it to Jennifer.

The toy looked up at her, blinked its oversized eyelashes, and snuggled into her chest.

Jennifer shrieked with delight and rocked the thing backwards and forwards in her arms.

"Ho. Ho. Ho. Happy Christmas, Jennifer," said Santa in his low voice, and led her to the door still clutching tightly to the toy. "Happy Christmas".

Jennifer's mother took her free hand and led her away. The mom behind her was just pushing her kid inside the grotto door and shouted across.

"It's all very clever stuff, but not the way I remember it."

Jennifer was holding the little horse up to her mother.

"Look what Father Christmas gave me."

"Yes dear, but you told me you don't believe in Father Christmas," mused the mother.

"Oh, yes," muttered Jennifer, "I don't. Anyway, it was only a silly old hologram."

As they walked off into the crowd, Jennifer left a trail of wet footprints on the mall's marble floor.

Lux

As it looked down on the city, the creature's many eyes could see sights that it had never seen before. Its wings beat in a flurry of iridescent splendour as it flapped down between the tall glowing structures from the black night sky.

It was hungry. Could there be nourishment in this strange place? Ahead was a vista of alien beauty. A network of buildings and interconnecting pathways vanished into the dark horizon. The creature knew that where there was light, there was life; where there was life, there was food.

The landscape was still. Nothing moved. But through the air was a constant, low penetrating hum.

Many of the buildings were opalescent vertical cylinders. Inside, the creature could just discern the outline of their basic structures with metal support columns and circular horizontal platforms. The light that came from inside was a combination of a dull orange and a piercing blue that spilled out on to the silver highways between.

Punctuating the taller structures were other cylinders, less luminous than the first. They were mostly a metallic blue colour that glinted and fluoresced in the darkness. Beside them, smaller cylinders with coloured bands seemed to be fixed into the ground with metal rods at each end.

Then the creature saw something it did not understand. Through a gaping circular hole in the ground it flew, to be confronted by ... the same. A subterranean city identical to the first, including the hole in the ground that led to ... another ... and another.

In the air, for the first time, it could smell what it was looking for. Sustenance. It could see the underside of the city above. It could see the vast complex of interconnecting pipes that joined building to building. Somewhere in the near vicinity was food and the marvels that were unfolding soon became insignificant to its prime objective.

There it was, just waiting to be eaten. Inviting. Unprotected. Now it would eat its fill. It circled a few times over the hoard and glided in with six legs braced. As its first two feet touched the knobbly ground, there was a blinding flash.

The creature's body arched in agony as a bolt of raw, blue energy shot through its body - ripping its very life away.

Jim Thompson slid a heavy rack back into the calculating machine and tightened the retaining screws.

"Did you find out what was wrong", said his assistant.

"Yes", laughed the electronics engineer, dropping the semi-disintegrated body of a moth into the waste basket.

He winked.

"Everything should be alright now; it was just a bug in the computer."

# Star Rock

"Hamish, come back here," shouted Alex Duncan. His West Highland White Terrier was some way along the sandy beach sniffing amongst some bladder wrack.

"Hamish, here boy," he called again and whistled, but the Westie was totally engrossed in something and paid no attention whatsoever.

Alex strolled along the foreshore. He was used to Hamish's obstinate behaviour by now.

"What have you found this time?" he asked.

Hamish was pawing at something and barking.

"What is it, a crab?" asked Alex.

Hamish had found crabs before and discovered to his displeasure that they nipped.

"Let's have a look," said Alex pushing Hamish aside with his foot. Hamish was getting quite agitated by this time.

It looked like a perfectly ordinary beach rock. It was dark grey granite like many of the other rocks on the beach – or was it? No, it had a different texture from granite, it was smoother with a metallic sheen, but it wasn't the texture that caught Alex's eye. It was the fact that the object was floating three inches off the ground!

Alex did a double-take. He got down on his knees and looked underneath to see if there was something hidden that was supporting it. No.

There was nothing but thin air between the 'rock' and the beach. Alex stood up and scratched his head. Hamish cowered back.

Alex touched the rock with his foot. He found

that he could push it sideways quite easily. It was obviously heavy, but there was no friction, so it floated along the beach like a curling stone on ice. Hamish ran after it barking.

*I had better report this*, he thought, but who would he report it to? Was it a job for the police? He wasn't sure. He decided to go and knock on the door of Donald McKay, the local schoolmaster.

"Donald, I've found something very peculiar on the beach just now. I was just taking Hamish for a walk and … no, this is going to sound ridiculous, you a had better come and take a look for yourself."

Donald put on his coat and followed Alex the few hundred yards down to the shore.

"It's over here," said Alex pointing. Hamish was already there and barking.

"Oh, my goodness," said Donald. "What could it be?" Alex asked, demonstrating the lack of friction.

Donald tried for himself.

"I've never seen anything like it," he exclaimed. "I can only think that it is something to do with the military. There is a base just down the coast on the mainland."

"Military?" said Alex in horror. "And here's me kicking it about like a football. It could have blown my leg off."

"I think that we had better give somebody a call," said Donald. "And keep your dog away from it in case it goes off."

Donald picked-up his handset and dialled 999.

"Which service, caller?"

"Oh, police, yes, put me through to the police," he replied.

A few minutes later, Donald put the phone down and went into the kitchen.

"Would you like a cup of tea, Alex? It's a bit early for a wee dram."

"Yes, tea would be fine, thanks, Donald. Did they say how long they would be?"

"They said that they would send someone round right away. It's not as if they are rushed off their feet in this place."

Ten minutes later, Sergeant Tam McFarlane pulled-up in his spotless white police car.

"Hello Tam," said Donald. "Alex has found something on the beach. He wasn't sure if it was a job for the police or army but you were the closest."

"What is it, Alex? Unexploded ordinance?"

Alex looked at Donald.

Donald shook his head.

"Damned if I know. It looks like a rock."

"A rock?" said Tam. "You mean that you called me out to a rock?"

"No, it's not a rock. It looks like a rock, but it floats," said Donald.

"What, you found something that floats on a beach. The tide washes stuff in all the time. What's so special about this?"

"You don't understand, Tam. It doesn't float on the sea, it floats on the land," piped Alex.

"Have you two been on the bottle at this time in the morning?" asked the policeman.

"Tam, you are not going to believe this until you see for yourself. Come with us," said Donald.

Down on the beach, Tam too had to get down on his knees and peer under the floating rock.

"Is it military?" asked Donald. "I think it is."

"I don't know," answered Tam. "I have no idea what it is but there's no knowing what they are up to at that base up the coast."

Tam went back to his car and got on the radio. He was on it for several minutes.

"They are sending someone over," said Tam. "They said not to touch it and keep people well clear of the beach."

"So, it is a bomb?" asked Donald.

"He didn't say that, he just said to keep people away from it. Better safe than sorry."

It was almost an hour before an inflatable boat turned up at the beach with three uniformed men in it. By this time, there was a small crowd standing behind the railings along the beach craning their necks to see what all the fuss was about. The military people inspected the rock, scratched their heads, and got on their walkie-talkies.

"Do you know what it is," asked Tam.

"Look, just keep these people back. It's your job to keep them safe. We will deal with this."

The military technician listened to the rock with a stethoscope. He looked at it with a magnifying glass, stood up, and shrugged.

"It's not one of ours," he said to his crew. "Don't know what it is or where it came from. I don't think it is ordinance. I think that we had better take it back with us and let the boffins have a look."

They wrapped the rock in a canvas sheet and carried it back to the RIB. Alex, Donald and Tam watched them disappear into the horizon.

In a laboratory hidden deep beneath a hill near Loch Lomond, four figures surrounded a bench. Two wore white lab coats, one a sharp suit and the other, a senior officer's uniform.

"What do we know about it?" asked Amir Turani rhetorically. "Let me begin by telling you what it isn't. Yes, it has all the physical appearances of a sea-worn granite rock. It's the size of a rock and has an irregular shape too, but our geologists have dismissed that possibility. No known type of rock has the properties that this has. As you can see, it repulses gravity the way that two similar magnetic poles push each other apart. We have x-rayed it and it is solid all the way through. We have analysed its composition with a mass spectrometer and with x-ray diffraction and have hit a brick wall. The material is just not known to science."

"Is it Russian?" asked the suit from the MOD.

"Very unlikely," said Turani.

"How did it end up on a beach on Islay?" asked the officer.

"I think it floated there," replied Turani. "We put the thing into a tank of water and it repelled the water by about seventy-five millimetres all round. It didn't sink, it floated in a depression on the surface of the water."

The young woman in the lab coat piped in. "As there was a volume of air surrounding it, its average density was less than the water it displaced, so it was buoyant. The same principle that allows metal ships to float."

"So, it could have been washed-in from anywhere?" asked the politician.

"Yes. We have palm trees growing on the west coast of Scotland thanks to the Gulf Stream. Viable seeds wash across the Atlantic in the warm currents and take root along the shoreline."

"Okay," said the officer, "you have told us what the object isn't. Have you any idea what it is?"

"Ah, I was afraid that you were going to ask me that," smiled Turani. "Yes, I know exactly what it is."

The suited man raised his eyebrows in anticipation. The officer cocked his head sideways and waited.

"It's an enigma. That's what it is. I don't have any proof but I would say that it fell from the skies, landed in the sea and got caught-up in the Gulf Stream Drift."

"You are saying that it is extra-terrestrial in origin?" asked the officer.

"Well," replied Turani, "it is certainly not of this world."

"I think that it needs to be taken down to London," said the MOD man.

That night, it left in an unmarked white van with a discrete police escort.

Amir Turani travelled south in a police escort vehicle. The seven-hour drive took them to a MOD laboratory on the outskirts of London.

"I've been dying to see this," said Mathew Carr, head of research. "By the way, thank you for the email, Amir. Most helpful."

Carr walked all around the object on the table and passed his hand underneath.

"Mmm," he muttered and removed his spectacles.

"Have you tried cutting it?" he asked Turani.

"Yes, our diamond tip drills wouldn't even scratch the surface," he replied. "It is not magnetic and does not react with any chemical we have tried, including very concentrated acids. It shows no sign of radioactivity. As far as I can tell, it is totally inert."

"And, you believe it's extra-terrestrial in origin?" asked Carr.

"I can't think of any other explanation," said the Iranian scientist.

"Well, I have a few more tests in mind," said Carr. "You will hang around?"

"Oh, most certainly," said Turani. "I am totally involved. It's my baby, as you might say."

With more sophisticated equipment at their

disposal, Matthew Carr and his team went to work with Turani looking on.

"It only has the mass of a common terrestrial granite rock but a sustained burn with a high-powered laser has had no effect whatsoever. It just soaked-up the energy. A minute afterwards, it was back at room temperature," explained Carr. "If we put a heavy weight on top of it, it is pushed closer to the table but immediately springs back up again when the weight is removed."

Carr put his hands on his hips.

"I'm completely kerflummoxed, and I don't mind admitting it."

"So, what can we do now?" asked Turani.

There's only one thing we can do," said Carr. "NASA!"

Amir Turani had always wanted to go to Texas, and now he was coming into land at Bush International Airport, Huston, ready for the short helicopter hop to NASA's Lyndon B Johnson Space Center. As he looked down on the rows of parked cars, he thought how different it looked from the approach to Glasgow Airport. It was greener than he imagined. The drive to the laboratory was lined with palm trees. The site itself was punctuated with rockets pointing up at the sky, but they were tourist attractions, rather than space-ready vehicles.

He was dropped-off at the front door of a large white building and wandered into reception carrying his luggage. The receptionist asked him to have a seat while somebody came to fetch him. He was given a visitors pass and looked round with interest at the historic photographs on the wall.

A chatty young woman took him in the lift to the seventh floor. She detected his Scottish accent and claimed to have Scottish ancestry but had never visited. He was shown in to a meeting room where three people were already waiting.

"Mister Turani, glad to know you," said the man in a waistcoat. "I am Dr Cole Weaver and my colleagues here are Dana Latter and Pablo Jiménez." The two nodded.

"I am intrigued by what I have been told about your find," said Dr Weaver, glancing down at a sheet of paper in front of him. He nodded as he scanned it.

"Very interesting."

"Can I just ask you something?" asked the rather stern looking woman. "You say that you have run every possible test on this object. You surmise that it could be a meteorite yet we have never come across anything in our explorations that remotely resembles it. Have you discovered what makes it levitate?"

"I can only guess that it repulses gravity." He brought his fingers together and then moved them apart to demonstrate.

She continued. "Do you have any idea of the significance of this discovery, the possibilities?"

Turani was a scientist, and a good one, but he hadn't even thought about 'possibilities'.

On the way down in the lift to the basement laboratory, Amir was plied with more questions by all three Americans. He could only answer some of them factually, whilst the rest of his answers were speculative.

In the lab, the rock was sitting in a shallow disk, just floating there like it always did. Several white-coated people were tapping it, pushing it downwards and letting it bounce up again. They photographed it and videoed its bounce against a graduated backdrop.

"All very low tech experiments," explained Dr Weaver. "The more serious stuff starts tomorrow."

*Yes, more serious stuff,* thought Amir Turani as he was shown into a large laboratory like he had never seen - not outside a science fiction movie anyway.

"What is it?" he asked the stern woman.

"It's just a small version of what you have at CERN," she said. "A particle accelerator. We are going to hit this thing with high energy charged particles to see what happens. It's only a small machine but if we don't get anything interesting, we will have to take it to Fermilab near Chicago."

"You are putting a lot of effort into this," said Amir. "You must have bottomless purses."

"I don't know about bottomless," grinned Pablo Jiménez, "but you don't get to play with one of these every day."

For the first time, Dana Latter cracked a slight

smile.

"Yes, if we can find out what makes this thing tick, it would be worth a lot of money."

"Money for whom?" asked Amir.

"NASA, of course," replied the woman.

"Strictly speaking, it was found on Scottish soil, it is the property of the People of Scotland," insisted Amir.

Latter dismissed the idea with a wave of her hand.

"There's a lot of work to do before we start sharing the spoils."

The experiments with the particle collider produced some results at last. It wasn't much, but bathing the rock in a stream of high energy particles for a few minutes caused it to increase its levitation by four millimetres – for a few minutes. It then sank back to its old position.

"We gotta get this over to Fermilab," said Latter. "Can you get this crated-up. I'll tell them we are on our way."

The director at Fermilab wasn't so enthusiastic about the request. They already had a backlog of work lined-up for universities all over the USA. NASA had no right to jump the line. Dana Latter pulled strings, she was good at that. A telephone call from someone higher up the chain soon made some experimental time available.

Amir was somewhat taken aback at how the

Americans casually used 'airplanes' like buses. He and Dana were on a plane to Chicago O'Hare by mid-afternoon in a NASA Lear Jet. The crate was tied-down in the cabin with them.

Dana opened-up when they were together alone. Her frostiness disappeared when they discussed their (unclassified) research projects. Amir had Iranian parents, but he was a Glaswegian through and through. Some of his expressions caught Dana off guard, but they got on just fine.

A large 4x4 was waiting to transport Amir, Dana, and their precious cargo to the Fermilab facility. Amir had seen photos of the iconic Wilson Hall building with its two bent, up thrusting towers. It was even more spectacular than he envisaged.

They were met by a reception committee. The crate was loaded onto a small flat truck and whisked away.

Amir was surprised to find that the head of research was an Englishman – Dr Leo Bradley. Bradley had kept his English accent, mostly. There were just a few words that came across as American. He was a little stand-offish, probably because he had been forced into this project by a superior and was a bit narked. When the object of the interruption to his day-to-day work was explained, he loosened-up considerably. He even showed interest.

Dana explained her experiment with their mini-particle accelerator at Johnson and told Bradley what she wanted to do and what she expected to happen. Bradley told them that they couldn't start right away. There was an important experiment in progress and it would be a couple of days before they could be fitted-in. He suggested some sightseeing.

Chicago offers a wealth of attractions and cultural centres. Dana had seen it all before and made some suggestions. Amir was a scientist at heart. He didn't have a great deal of interest in museums and art galleries. His great passion outside work was cricket. He wasn't going to be humoured here. Dana asked him if he would like to see a baseball game, after all, baseball is just like cricket. He thought about it for a moment.

"No, I wouldn't understand it," he said. "The rules are too different and I don't know a thing about baseball."

So, they grabbed a taxi and told the driver to show them the sights. It was all on NASA expenses so Dana didn't have to worry about the cost.

Over dinner that night, Amir and Dana talked about personal things. Amir was still a bachelor and shared a house with three other guys. Dana was divorced, twice, and avowed never to marry again. Their lives couldn't have been more different. Amir was wedded to his work and had only left Scotland on a handful of occasions. On the other hand, Dana had been a globetrotter both through work and on vacation.

After another day of looking round Chicago, and a baseball game at Wrigley Field, they were told that Fermilab was ready for them. The rock had been loaded into a chamber with a mass of sensors and ultra-high-speed cameras. The chamber was sealed and the building evacuated. Amir and Dana were in the air-conditioned control room with Leo Bradley and a host of technicians. It was just a fraction too cold for Amir. He had no trouble with the heat outside, despite being Scottish.

It seemed to take ages for the accelerator to be prepped and wound-up. The control room was a mass of monitors with scrolling numbers, but a couple of them featured his rock overlaid with a grid of lines.

"We will be monitoring its mass and levitation," explained Leo Bradley. "Of course, what you see on the monitor is in real time but it is being filmed at two hundred and fifty thousand frames per second. Keep your eyes on the readouts here," he said, pointing at a screen. "We will be starting in two minutes."

He turned and nodded at one of the technicians.

"Mark," he said.

Amir watched the countdown on the monitor. When it reached zero, his rock started to glow.

"It's just soaking-up the energy like a sponge," said the technician. "I'm increasing the power."

"It's levitating," shouted Dana Latter. "Look."

The grid on the screen showed that the rock was

rising slowly. It was nearly white hot by now and they were still increasing the feed of high energy particles.

"It has increased its mass tenfold," said another technician.

"Wind it down," instructed Leo Bradley. "I think we have enough for now."

Amir took a deep breath. It was cold in the control room but his forehead was covered in sweat.

"Now, all we have to do is study the results," said Bradley.

"How long is that going to take?" asked Dana.

"Mmm. A couple of days probably."

Amir baulked at the idea of two more days with Dana in a taxi.

Amir and Dana were summoned into Leo's office.

"I have some interesting results to show you," said Leo turning his monitor around to give them a better view.

"As you saw for yourself, the rock absorbed everything we threw at it. It glowed for a while but as soon as we switched-off the particle beam, it cooled down again almost instantly. Its levitation also fell back to normal. It did, however, retain its increased mass. It is now ten times heavier than it was when we started. Somehow, it has converted all that energy into mass. Now, if we had some way to convert that mass back into energy, we would have the big daddy of all batteries.

"Really," said Dana with a glint in her eyes.

"Unfortunately," said Leo, "we don't possess such technology."

"Can we experiment a bit more?" asked Amir.

"Sorry, you have already put our schedule way behind. We can't afford any more time at present. You could contact CERN, but you might have to wait a couple of years. I think they are down at the minute."

Leo's phone rang. He picked it up.

"Really?" he said and listened some more.

"Thanks, Randy," he said replacing the receiver.

"Seems that they have something even more interesting to show us down at the lab," said Leo, beckoning.

In the computer room, a young technician was setting up a large monitor.

"Please have a seat," he said. "As you are aware, we had an ultra-high-speed camera setup recording the experiment. I have to explain, our cameras are not designed for this kind of work, we tend to work at a much smaller scale. However, I think you will find this playback of interest."

The others were agog.

"We saw the object take on a certain luminosity. To the human eye, it was just a glow. Now, slowed down two hundred and fifty thousand times, we can see that it is not a steady glow, but a series of pulses. You expect a light bulb to give a steady glow but it is actually fluctuating at sixty times a second. Human persistence of vision interprets this as a steady illumination. The eyes can't see the flicker. Now, if you were to film a light bulb with a high speed camera, it would be very clear that it was going on and off sixty times a second. There is a degree of thermal inertia going on, admittedly, but it is not a constant illumination. Now, coming back to our experiment. The object's flickering is at a much higher frequency than 60Hz, but it is flickering."

"And what does that tell us?" asked Amir.

"Quite a lot, actually," said the technician. "When we were able to establish the clock rate, we found that the flickering was not random. It was a binary sequence."

"You mean it was counting?" asked Dana, open-mouthed. "What was it counting?"

"It went through all the prime numbers from 2 up to 997. Then it stopped briefly and repeated itself. There was a lot of other stuff that made no sense but the series of prime numbers tells us something very significant!"

"Intelligence?" proffered Dana.

"It would seem so," said the technician.

The room went silent.

"Is there some way we can decode the rest of this information?" asked Dana. "Can I take it back to Johnston and put our computers on it? We have people who are experts in this."

The technician smiled.

"You want a copy on a USB stick?"

He tapped the glass of the partition between the meeting room and the computer suite next door.

There was a bank of mainframe computers winking and blinking.

"We have a recording about five seconds long and it takes that lot to store and process it. Five megapixels times two hundred and fifty thousand frames per second, you do the math."

"We have some pretty serious kit at NASA too, you know," said Dana.

"Yes, I am aware of that," said the technician. "And, you are welcome to share the data. I am just pointing out that getting all those Exabyte's across to your computers at Houston is going to take some time. Sending them over networks is inefficient because of the error rate. Sending the data physically on media is a probably a better bet if you have your own transport?"

"Yes, we have a Lear Jet waiting at O'Hare," said Dana.

"Perfect," said the technician. "I will have the data transferred to hard drives. There might be a few!"

The crate that held the rock was originally wheeled-in on a simple hand-trolley. It now needed a fork-lift truck to lift it. The racks of servers holding the data were bulky and heavy too. It was decided to use a cargo transport plane to move it all back to Houston. The Lear Jet couldn't cope with all that weight.

Space was found for the servers' racks and they were hooked-in to a computer suite in a NASA's laboratory.

When Dana and Amir went for a debrief, it was confirmed that the data did contain a sequence of prime numbers. They also found a long Fibonacci sequence and a representation of Pi to 256 decimal places. Even then, there was data that they did not understand. The data that could be deciphered and made sense represented less than a hundredth of a second. There were two seconds of data.

Incomprehensible data!

Leo Bradley forwarded the data to his colleague, Noah Watkins at SETI. After a bit of toing and froing, they came to an inevitable and momentous conclusion.

"Ladies and Gentlemen," said Leo Bradley to the gathered press. "Something has happened in the past few days that we have been waiting for, waiting for a lifetime. As you know, we have been searching the skies for a hint of another civilisation. We have plotted stars that are similar to our own sun along with their planets that orbit in what we call the 'Goldilocks Zone'. We have listened for signals with our radio telescopes and diligently scoured the surfaces of planets in our own solar system in the hope that we might find just the smallest clue that would suggest that we are not alone. The Universe is a lonely place. We have, so far, not found any such clues in the heavens."

A muttering began in the assembled crowd. Leo waved for quietness.

"Now, it seems, we have been looking in the

wrong place with the wrong equipment."

He took a deep breath.

"I am very honoured to be able to announce today that our search for extra-terrestrial life, and I meant sentient extra-terrestrial life, has come to fruition. We have, on our own world, made first contact!"

There was an uproar in the hall. Reporters were shouting out questions and falling over each other to get near to the podium.

Leo continued with an up-stretched hand. "We will be passing out a press release detailing our findings. At this point in time, we have no further information to give you. Please bear with us until we have more detailed information.

The press fought for interviews, but were rejected. Leo and Dana disappeared into a back room and the door was locked. Amir was standing over to the side hoping that no-one would accost him for information. He was there as an observer only. Luckily, nobody made the connection.

The headlines in the newspapers next day were almost identical.

"FIRST CONTACT!"

What followed the headline was a mixture of rife speculation and ignorance. Nothing but the basic fact was actually disclosed.

Amir, Dana and Leo sat round the meeting room

table. Leo had, in front of him, a laptop showing a screenful of numbers.

"We've had our best mathematicians go over these figures but they can't shed any light on the bulk of the data. There are the obvious stand-out sequences and they did find one more obscure sequence that I don't understand myself. The rest is a mystery."

Dana rubbed her hand across the surface of the table.

"If we sent a message to another civilisation that was to show that we are intelligent, we would do exactly the same thing. Mathematics must be the same across the universe. It all comes down to how many digits you have on your hands. We have ten fingers so we have adopted a decimal method of counting. If ET has twelve fingers or sixteen, they would use base twelve or base sixteen. They must have fingers or they couldn't build things. Binary only requires noughts and ones so can be used by anybody. It's the lowest common denominator."

"Could the non-numerical data be letters?" asked Amir. "Letters from a language that we don't understand."

"There wouldn't be much point in communicating something that the recipient is unlikely to understand," said Dana. "I never saw the point of sending CD-ROMs on space missions. The aliens are unlikely to have a CD-ROM player."

"What," said Amir, "if the data was not intended for us at all. What if it was a message to their own kind?"

Leo and Dana pondered.

"I see what you are getting at," said Dana. "Kind of 'ET phone home'."

As they struggled with the concept, a knock was heard at the door. A women stuck her head round and beckoned to Leo Bradley. She whispered in his ear. His arms went limp. He turned to the other two.

"You are not going to believe this. The crate with the rock in it was put in a high security storage facility last night. When they went to check it this morning, the crate was empty. It was still sealed, but completely empty."

Jaws dropped.

In the middle of the previous night, a small spacecraft had materialised over the NASA secure storage facility. It hadn't zoomed-down from space, it just appeared.

A tight beam of energy was projected downwards. It passed through the roof and into the crate. The atoms in the rock set up a sympathetic resonance with something in the craft above. Energy waves intertwined with the molecular structure of the object. It became nebulous. As the waves rippled and modulated, the rock passed though the solid lid of the box and through the roof of the warehouse. It rose through the air and was swallowed by the hovering craft. It vanished immediately. The entire process took, perhaps, a thousandth of a second.

'Twix a rock and a Hard Place

It looked so very easy, the way the robot blasted the meteorites out of the sky as they curved in towards the domed city.

From his rocky pedestal a few hundred meters from the settlement, he constantly probed the starry sky with high precision sensors. Calculating their trajectories precisely, he could anticipate exactly where the rocks would hit. If they were a threat, he would spit twin beams of awesome laser energy from the cannons on his chest and they vaporised the rock instantly. It was fool proof.

Once a year, and to the day, there would be a lull in the perpetual bombardment from space - something to do with the alignment of the moons. The sentinel would be given a routine maintenance check and the human crew would disarm the lasers as a simple matter of safety. Nobody could be in the vicinity when one of those babes went off.

His drive systems were inoperative too. They were nuclear powered and threw up shields automatically in the presence of humans to protect them from radiation, but most of the robot's sensors still worked, and his brain still had low order functions - they could run off the back-up batteries for weeks.

The robot had been neutralised for just over an hour when it picked up an object coming in from space. It was big. It was fast. It would not hit the dome directly, no, but that mass and velocity would set off tremendous seismic shock waves. It was too close; it would be total obliteration!

The crew's small weapons would be useless against such a monster, even if they could hit it at that speed. The robot had no contact with them anyway - its communications modules were strewn all around him on the ground with a service mechanic almost lost in the innards. What could it do?

Another pressure-suited engineer had the weapons system dismantled and sitting on a diagnostic trolley. He was engrossed in the readouts and punched data into the computer.

The robot put its remaining circuits into overload. That brought on a cluster of flashing warning lights and sent a message racing across its external video monitor, but the crew were too busy, they had a job to do, and quickly. Through the vacuum of the airless world, they could not even hear its relays clicking out their Morse code warning of disaster. They would not have understood Morse code anyway.

Now the object was in visual range, the robot's visual range. By the time the humans saw it, it would be too late, but they were totally oblivious of the fast approaching doom.

The robot's mind was in turmoil. It was its only purpose to defend humankind from danger but it was powerless. A reflex action sent a feeble surge of power to its lasers but nothing happened because they weren't there. Now the target was a bright glowing mass plummeting downwards, they would all die. Its monitor and warning lights flickered wildly. Desperately.

Suddenly a crewman looked up and came running over. He put his hand into to a service panel and yanked a cable hard. The robot slumped.

"Phew! That was close. I had to pull the plug on this one," he called into his helmet mic. "I don't know what went wrong but by the look of these readings, it was about to blow any second."

"I shouldn't worry too much," called back a colleague. "It's due for a new cortex unit anyway and it should be on that relief ship just coming in now. Where's my screwdriver?"

# Flat Screen

Another alien ship exploded in a mass of flames.

The score increased by 100.

"How do the aliens get into the computer?" asked Jason's little brother.

"Same way all the little people get into the television, stupid. Have you never looked round the back?"

Michael shook his head, open mouthed.

"There's a little door in the back of the television set. They go in there at night when nobody is looking," explained Jason, with a straight face.

"Oh," said Michael, nodding slowly. "And the cars too?"

"Yes, the cars too. The little people drive them in."

Michael toddled over to the television and peered round the back inquisitively. He couldn't see anything.

Jason grinned mischievously. How could anybody be so gullible? He just had to tell his mates about this. It was so funny.

"Come away from the back of that television, Michael" shouted Tony Chandler. "It's dangerous."

"What, little people come out?" asked the child, open-eyed.

Tony wanted to re-enforce his warning without getting into the gruesome reality of electrocution.

"Yes, the little people will come out and get you," he half smiled.

Michael recoiled in horror and ran off to seek the protection of his mother, Marie, in the kitchen.

"What rubbish have you been telling Michael?" asked Marie with raised eyebrows and holding the sobbing urchin close to her.

"He has to learn that it is dangerous round there," said Tony. "What if he were to poke something into one of the ventilation holes? There are very high voltages in there."

"Michael, you must not go round the back of the television," said Marie, wagging a finger.

"Why?" he asked.

"Just don't that's all," scolded his mother.

"Tony, why do we still have that old television anyway? You promised to get a new one ages ago."

"It has a better picture than the new ones and there is nothing wrong with it," insisted her husband.

"I've seen Tom and Emma's new flat-screen television next door," said Marie. "It is much better than that one. Big screen, better sound and it cost a lot less that that old thing."

"I've looked at them in the shops," argued Tony. "Look along a row of them, they are all different. They should be identical but they aren't. Cheap rubbish churned out by robot assembly lines in the Far East. They don't build them like they used to. This one stays. It's good for a few years yet. It will probably still be working when the one next door is on the scrapheap."

Marie shook her head in indignant resignation and took Michael back to the kitchen.

149

"Dad, Michael thinks that there are little people inside the television. Isn't that funny?" said Jason.

"And, where did he get that idea from?" asked Tony.

"Don't know," lied Jason. "Anyway, how can you be sure that there are not?"

"Huh," said Tony. "Do you think I'm as stupid as Michael? Do you know how a television works, then?"

"No," snapped Jason accusingly, as if the question was unfair.

Later that afternoon, Jason went to his bedroom and pulled a box of toys from under his bed. He took some toy figures and some little vehicles, brought them downstairs and secreted them behind the television. He was going to have some fun at his little brother's expense.

"Michael, come and see," he shouted out through the patio doors. The child waddled in.

"Look what's behind the television," he continued, pointing at the set.

Michael went over to the television and looked round the back. His jaw dropped.

"Little people," he cried.

"Must have got shut out," grinned Jason. "Now that it's daytime, they can't move. They are trapped outside."

Michael looked over at him pitifully.

"Little people can't get in?" he asked.

"Aww," said the smaller boy sympathetically.

After supper, it was getting time for Michael to go to bed. Tony had gone out to see a man about a dog. Jason was upstairs doing his homework. Marie was running a bath for Michael, who was still playing in the living room. He toddled over to the television and peered round the back. The little toy figures were still there. He reached round and grabbed a metal toy soldier. Finding a ventilation slot, he tried to push the toy soldier through. The slot was too narrow but the soldiers rifle snapped off and fell down inside the television.

"Michael, your bath's ready," said Marie, walking into the room with a towel across her arm.

"Didn't I tell you to stay away from the back of that television?" she scolded.

"Little people," said Michael, pointing.

"Come and get your bath," said Marie whipping him into her arms. "Who is telling you this nonsense?"

"Daddy," said the boy.

Marie's eyes went up to the ceiling.

Tony pulled a bottle of beer from the fridge, twisted-off the cap, and sat down in the living room. He picked-up the TV remote and pushed the standby button. He waited. Nothing happened.

He got up from his sofa and went over to the television. He banged hard on the top with his fist. Nothing happened. He pressed the main power button on an off a few times. There was a flash and a bang and the smell of acrid smoke.

"What the hell was that?" said Marie, running into the room.

"I think there's something wrong with the television," said Tony, with a hit of embarrassment.

"Oh, we can get a new one then?" she said expectantly.

"No, I will get this one fixed. I'm sure that it's just something simple like a fuse."

"How much?" screamed Tony down the phone. "You must be kidding."

The television repair man at the other end had obviously had that same reaction many times before and started to explain…

"Look, it's an old model," he explained. "Parts are hard to come by now. I can only get them from one source and they can charge whatever they like. They have the monopoly. The main board is gone, that's 300. It also took the power supply with it. That's another 150. Then, there's the labour…"

"Can't you just fix it up to last a bit longer, it's a good set?" asked Tony.

"No, you can't fix televisions at a component level these days," said the man. "I can only do a complete board swap."

"I can get a brand new set for less than you quoted," complained Tony.

"Yes, you can. I'm sorry, it's just the way things are now."

Tony bought a new 40" television.

Marie was very happy.

� � �

Their childhood sibling rivalry far behind them, Jason and Michael became the best of buddies. Jason's girlfriend, Tina, had invited Michael over for dinner along with his new girlfriend, Lauren.

Lauren was a stunner, if a bit liberal with the eye makeup and lipstick. Jason didn't know how his little brother had landed a catch like this. Michael introduced her.

"Jason and Tina, this is my friend, Lauren."

"Hi, Lauren. Nice to meet you. Have you known Michael for very long?" asked Tina.

"Nah, just a week. We met down the pub."

"Really," said Tina. She didn't take to Lauren's accent.

Michael played the perfect suitor. He offered Lauren a drink. She wanted vodka. He pulled out the chair for her at the dining table and pushed it in when she sat down. She knocked-back the vodka in one gulp and held out her glass ungraciously for another.

"Really good spag bol," said Michael.

"Yes," agreed Lauren. "Wish I could cook like that."

"It was only spaghetti Bolognese," blushed Tina. "It doesn't get any simpler than that."

"She even has trouble with a takeaway," joked Michael. Lauren didn't see anything funny about it and scowled at him with clenched lips.

Jason could sense the bad vibes and decided to lighten it up.

"Hey, have you seen the story today about the flying saucer landing in China?"

"Aw, Jason, you don't believe all that stuff. It's utter nonsense. Guys with nothing better to do than fake stupid UFO sightings just to get clicks on their web page."

"Oho, you're talking about me," said Jason. "Who was it that believed that there were little people inside our television set? Huh? Mister Smarty Ass."

Michael showed a modicum of embarrassment.

"I was three years old then, you sod!"

They all laughed.

When the after dinner conversation got round to what everybody did for a living, Lauren looked at her blingy watch, pulled Michael's arm and told him that she had to go.

Michael and Lauren broke it off two days later. Whether it was Michael's realisation that she couldn't cook or Lauren's notion that Michael wasn't the alpha male she was looking for, it didn't matter. They went their own ways.

The next time that Michael brought a girl round for dinner at Jason and Tina's place, it became immediately clear that Alexa was a different class of lady altogether. She helped Tina with the salad and laying the table. She asked for Soave.

Later, Michael was helping Tina load the

dishwasher in the kitchen. Jason and Alexa were flicking through his music collection on the television screen.

"Michael, I've been meaning to ask you. Did you really believe that there were little people inside the television? I mean, I know that you were only three but did you really believe all that stuff?"

"Yes, I did," mused Michael. "I believed it because I had imagination. I could see those little people and their cars. I could see them open the flap on the back of the set and go inside. Then, when the television was switched on, I could see them again, on the screen. Exactly the same people."

Tina smiled a false smile, wondering if he was mad.

Michael tried very hard to keep a straight face, but he felt it was beginning to crack.

He winked and laughed.

Tina hit him across the ear with a dishcloth.

"Michael Chandler, you … you're just as bad as your brother!"

Michael waved his hand to calm her down.

"I was playing next door with David and I hear my mum talking about the television with David's mum. My mum said that my dad was too mean to buy a new television. I didn't really understand all this but I did know that my mum would really love to have a new television like theirs. I couldn't buy one for her, I was only three."

Michael looked down at the floor sheepishly.

"But I got one for her anyway."

# A Day in the Life
# of a Leg of a Chair

One day, a new awareness dawned and discovered to its dismay that it was the chromium plated leg of a pretty ordinary chair, and a back leg at that.

Now, being the hind leg of a chair, there was not a lot it could do about it, but it could think – therefore it was!

When it took stock of its immediate surroundings, it came to realise that it was standing in a highly automated car factory, its sole purpose to support a human being who 'minded' the machines from a small master control console.

There was a time when the human would sit all day, reading his newspaper, doing the crosswords and periodically dozing off, but now he had gone. Nothing ever went wrong. Somehow his chair had stayed in the same place, forgotten.

Now the reason that nothing ever went wrong is that the machines were self-repairing. As soon as a circuit would blow, or a bearing would seize, the master control would detect it and instantly switch-in a back-up unit. Robot maintenance units would move in and replace the faulty part and it would then, in turn, become a back-up unit.

The chances of a back-up developing a fault before the robots could replace the original were astronomical. But when this did eventually happen one day, it was inside the master control console itself!

All down the line, the robot arms went out of sequence. They started drilling holes where holes shouldn't be and putting bolts into holes that weren't there. The paint arms were spraying car shells in multi-coloured mixtures. The seats were being fitted back to front. Door panels were being attached to the roof.

Oh, if only the machine minder was still here!

At the end of the assembly line, there should have been shinning new cars neatly stacked for the delivery trucks. Instead there were heaps of multi-coloured abstract sculptures with four oddly placed wheels, winking headlights and rotating wing mirrors. Had there been just one of these objects, it might have been a delightful conversation piece in some art gallery, and probably quite valuable. Coming off the assembly line at a rate of one a minute, there was definitely a market glut by any reasoning.

Oh, if only the machine minder was still here!

The chair leg was bewildered. It wished that it could communicate with its three companions, but did not even know if they too could think. What could it do? It could not move, or shout, or radio for assistance. Basically, it was 400 millimetres of tubular mild steel with a rubber foot at one end and a three-holed flange at the other. The possibilities were very limited.

Oh, if only the machine minder was still here!

By this time, the loading bay was half full of grotesque mechanical monsters with flailing windscreens and transmission shafts. Like psychedelic windmills, they whirled their misplaced appendages in the air. Alternately, they snapped off in showers of sparks or got caught up with the next and caused the main body to rotate instead. Each time another one joined the melee, the sound of tortured, grinding steel and splintering glass would add to the pandemonium.

The chair leg had to do something. It had a responsibility. It was after all, a machine minder's chair.

Sending out a stream of consciousness, it could sense every atom of its being. It concentrated hard. It was the leg of a chair, it could think, surely it could do something. It focussed energetically on its own being. Its molecules started to vibrate.

"Heat", it thought, "Heat."

As the molecules became excited, they caused internal friction. The friction made the temperature rise inside the metal.

The chair leg glowed a dull red.

It concentrated even harder.

It got brighter. Red. Orange. Yellow.

With a final surge, the chair leg brought all its existence to bear.

It glowed white hot. Just like the ingot that it was originally made from.

Suddenly, the sprinkler system cut in. Everything stopped. Like the falling note of a siren, the electric motors all slowed down in unison until the only sound was the pitter-patter of water spraying on bare metal panels.

The factory inspector half laughed, half cried when he saw the mad cacophony of semaphore in the loading bay. He sat down on a chair beside the main control consul in total disbelief and scratched his head. He did not notice that one chair leg had blistered, flaking chromium plating and an almost imperceptible curved crease that for all the world looked like a smug grin.

# Warworld

The white dot in the black sky grew larger. It resolved into a sleek silver triangle and silently dropped down into the mists of Metulia.

The sensors showed a surface temperature of minus two hundred degrees and an atmospheric pressure of two thousand pounds per square inch. Not what you would call a comfortable environment, but then nobody ever visited this warworld, nobody human that is.

Metulia had been nominated by the Galactic Federation as a battleground. An arena where feuding sides could settle their differences without harming innocents or neutrals. All-out war was a thing of the past, yet differences had to be settled somehow.

There was still pride.

The glider skidded to a halt amidst a wake of white dust, having dug a furrow some two miles long in the frozen planet's surface. It would never rise again; it was strictly a one-way trip. It would have fulfilled its purpose.

The reverberations that rung round the hull ceased and a new sound came from within. The front of the thin dart opened like the mouth of some gigantic fish and from the dimly-lit depths emerged a glistening silver figure floating on a gravity platform.

Vem was the champion of the people of Andra. Like a knight in shining armour from some ancient book, he glided down the ramp onto the cold surface. Here, he was to represent his people in mortal combat. With what or whom, he did not know. He was tasked with winning this war for his people single-handedly and that he would do to the best of his ability. Only his head penetrated the low blanket of swirling gasses that covered the valley floor. Tall jagged mountains surrounded him on three sides; to the front, there was nothing ... a white nothing.

The land fell away and merged with the sky as he swept forwards on his gravity platform. He was clearly in a box canyon and his enemy could only approach from one direction. It was a good strategy. He was protected to the rear and flanks by the mountains, so he focussed all his sensors in the direction that mattered, and hibernated.

It was three chronospans before the message came down from the sky relay to waken him. The orbiting satellite was the referee that would monitor the duel, ever vigilant against any attempt by either side to circumvent the rules of battle.

"Both champions are now present on the warworld, let battle commence. May the best side win."

Vem switched all his sensing power to maximum sensitivity and probed the horizon.

Nothing.

The mountains surrounding him were blocking his line-of-sight radar so he launched a hover-eye far into the black sky far above his head. From above, his hover-eye could see himself far below. He could also see the glider and the long trench it had dug reaching out into the plain beyond the canyon. He could see the horizon all around and scanned it slowly.

Suddenly, his instruments flickered wildly. His enemy was there, too distant to distinguish in detail, but advancing rapidly. He, at once, transmitted the challenge code and the reply came back almost instantly. He wondered. What was the foe that dared to challenge the Champion of Andra? Was it a sophisticated weapon from some highly advanced civilisation that could decimate him with its first energy bolt or a puny biological life form from an upstart world. He just did not know.

He would find out soon.

He put his energy shield on auto. It would engage in microsecond at the merest hint of attack. It could protect him from all but the very most advance weapons that his people possessed. His battery of plasma blasters and proton missiles could destroy a small moon if he wished.

He was ready.

The enemy was closing in, but still out of range. His hover-eye could just make out the disturbances in the terrain that betrayed the approaching opponent.

Vem had no fear, only a job to do: to smash the enemy, to win – but the victory would not be his.

The hover-eye could not move fast enough to dodge the almighty blast of heat that sent it burning from the sky. It plunged into the ground in a cloud of steam, leaving Vem startled, ashamed and almost blind. Could he shoot so accurately from that range? He hadn't tried. Was he foolish, he thought to himself, to assume that the enemy had similar capabilities to his own?

He then became aware of the missile arcing across the sky towards him. His auto-shield kicked-in. The missile hit it squarely but it deflected the blast effortlessly. Chunks of solid gas spread outwards in every direction. A smoking plume mushroomed into the sky. Should he reply with a missile of his own? He could trace the heat source of the enemy's missile back to its source but he suspected that his foe would no longer be there. Was this just a trick to deplete his strength?

The next incoming missile vaporised his gravity glider. What was the point of that? He soon found out when the glider's reactors exploded. He could feel the shock wave through the energy shield. At that instant he spotted the enemy's hover-eye dodging behind a peak behind him. He did a rapid calculation and released a missile to impact with a point on the peak directly below it. The explosion came seconds later from the top of the mountain. Had he hit it? No, the remote controlled drone hovered steadily in the shock wave like a surfer riding a wave. It was with a vengeance that he sent a barrage of plasma bolts into the hover eye. It disappeared in a cloud of smoke.

Now, they were even!

Night came. Vem's radar and infra-red sensors could normally cope with pitch darkness, but the raging storms that ripped the planet's surface at night rendered them virtually useless. The sky was thick with particles of solid gas. It was like a fog, an impenetrable fog. At least, the enemy would be in the same predicament.

He would be safe until sunrise. He slept.

As the sky lightened, the winds subsided, leaving a thick mist across the landscape. He could not even detect the mountains around him, but in the distance, he could just detect a metallic echo – then a stab of searing heat. The energy shield just flicked-on in time to deflect the worst of the blast. He fired a second missile at the radar echo but it had scarcely left the protective dome of his energy shield when it exploded in a blinding flash, hit by an accurately-placed energy bolt.

Vem floated forward towards his invisible foe, sending phalanxes of raw energy at where the enemy should be. He was very aware of the return fire bouncing off his shield and being absorbed by the hissing terrain. His barrage and the replies continued for ages.

Then, a warning flashed in his brain. His energy level monitor was telling him that he had passed the half-way mark and that his reserves were reaching critical. Using his shields like this was using as much power as his blasters. He had to try to hold fire and not waste energy.

Two more devastating bolts came from nearby. His shields sapped-up yet more precious energy. Then there was calm. The onslaught had stopped. He could see that a tunnel had been cut through the thick fog by the heat from the powerful energy weapons, and there, in full view, was his adversary.

It was like looking in a mirror. The other robot was identical to himself, ACKX6 robotic mercenary. Obviously, the enemy planet was also a low-tech world and had to buy its weapons from the same suppliers. It too had bought a basic frame and fitted it with power units, weapons, drives and sensors. It also had to programme the robot in battle tactics, to seek and destroy, but the fact remained: the two champions of their planets were effectively twins.

A quick playback of the last few hours gave Vem an exact inventory of missiles fired by both opponents and showed that, give or take a few units, the enemy's power reserves must be as low as his. Just enough, in fact, for one good shot with a plasma cannon or one deflection of the same. There were no missiles left.

He considered carefully.

If he fired first, his enemy might be able deflect and send a last broadside back at him. He wasn't that confident of his estimates but suspected that his shield strength would be insufficient to save him.

Oh, it didn't matter if he was physically destroyed, he was expendable and he knew it. Upholding his planet's honour was his prime directive. He could not let his side down. The enemy must fire first. He would deflect as best he could and use his last few megajoules of energy to destroy the other.

As time passed without event, he realised that as they were twins, his enemy must have come to the same conclusion.

The two metal figures stood facing each other, sensors on tight beam and high alert. Each waited for the ultimate blast that could leave the other defenceless.

Only victory would count.

Only annihilation of the foe was an acceptable outcome.

The mist rolled into the void between them. They stood there in the frozen wilderness and waited.

Waited.

Waited until their last joule had faded away to nothing.

# Future Perfect

When he awoke that morning, Midge Fuller had a pounding hangover. That was not unusual. When he opened his eyes, he was not in a bedroom that he recognised. That was not unheard of either. The fact that the room was a spotless, ultra-modern bedroom with a full wall window was not usual at all.

Who had he pulled last night?

He could remember virtually nothing of the previous evening. There was no sign of his … well, he had no idea if he had scored or not. There was no sign of anybody else in the room, nor indeed, that anyone else had been in the room. No clothes scattered across the floor haphazardly in a frenzy of passion. No empty glasses, bottles or coffee cups. No doner kebab polystyrene trays.

Through the fog that was his mind, he puzzled. Hauling himself over the edge of the bed, he stretched and yawned. Something caught his eye. He wandered over to the window in only his underpants. Through the window, he could see a vista of glistening skyscrapers disappearing off into the distance as far as the eye could see.

He gulped. This was not Wandsworth!

This was not anywhere that he recognised. In front of him were a myriad of tall glass and steel buildings. Above, strange aircraft criss-crossed the sky.

Midge shook his head hard from side to side and breathed deeply. What was going on?

He looked around the bedroom and spotted the door. It was pale green and flush with a wall of the same colour. There was no handle, only a dimple. He put his finger into the dimple and the door concertinaed open. He jumped back.

He rubbed his head. The hallway outside opened into a large living room ahead and a bathroom to the side. He decided to use the bathroom. It was not like any bathroom he had ever seen. He had heard of wet-rooms – posh people had them. The entire room was the shower. There was an odd contraption that must have been a toilet. As he approached it, the lid opened. It reminded him of the fancy toilets in planes. Then, there was something that looked like a hand basin except that it had no taps. He tried putting his hands into it. They were immediately surrounded by a soft white mist that seemed to move between his fingers. He shook his hands to get rid of the mist but it continued to gyrate for a full twenty seconds and then fell off into the basin and disappeared.

He had heard of hangovers being accompanied by pink elephants, but never anything like this.

Midge wandered into the living room. Everything looked very expensive, just as he had seen in pictures of film stars' houses. There were ultra-modern chairs and a glass sculpture that must have been a coffee table. In the corner, he noticed a kitchen dinette. He decided to look in the fridge. Nothing in the fridge looked familiar. No cans of lager, no half-eaten ready meals, no stale bread. He took out what looked like an ice tray. Instead of ice, it had something pink filling the compartments. He squeezed one out and tried it. It could have been frozen yoghurt, that was not something that he had ever tried, so he wasn't sure. It tasted sweet and fruity, so he ate it.

A shelf near the top of the fridge held a collection of plastic boxes. He pulled one out and opened the snap-on lid. He didn't know what was inside. It reminded him of the salads that they put in with his doner kebabs but there were round things amongst it. They looked a bit like nuts, but not any nuts he knew of. But then, he didn't have any experience of anything but salted peanuts. He put some of the food into his mouth with his fingers and took a slug of something pastel-coloured in a plastic bottle. It didn't taste too bad, but he had no idea what it was. He tried to put the plastic box back where it came from but he couldn't. Its place had been taken by another identical box. Where did that come from?

Midge looked around the room. It could have been a show-house. No sign of anyone living there, apart from the food in the fridge. He found another door in the room. It too had a dimple and he touched it. This time, the door split and slid sideways into the walls. Okay, he had never seen a door like this except in lifts. He wasn't stepping into a lift, was he? It looked like a hallway but didn't have any other doors. It was a lift. He felt the downwards movement and it certainly seemed to be going very fast. Suddenly, he started to feel heavier as the lift decelerated. It came to a halt, adjusted itself and the door split open.

Midge didn't know what to expect when the lift

doors opened, whatever it was, it wasn't this. In front
of him was a large foyer. It was milling with people
in an unfamiliar style of clothes. There were screens
floating in mid-air with animated advertisements
for products he had never heard of, each plying for
the attention of the people below. He could also see
figures that were not people. He had only ever seen
these things in the movies. Robots. Humanoid robots.

Midge's knees went weak. He shook his head
again in the hope of clearing the illusion and bringing
back his familiar Arndale Centre into focus.

No, robots it was!

He could feel eyes upon him. Everybody seemed
to be looking at him. Then, he realised that he was
still in only his underpants. He slid quickly behind a
pillar.

Looking back at the wall where the lift door was,
he could now see dozens of lift doors. He had no idea
which lift he had used or which floor he had come
from. He had no idea what he was going to do.

He felt a hand upon his shoulder. He wheeled
round.

"Hi Midge," said the girl. "Why did you come
down here like that?"

*Who the hell is she?* he said to himself, *and how does
she know my name?*

"I think I'm a bit lost," said Midge. "Where is
this?"

"Wandsworth," came the answer. "Where do you
think?"

Midge felt dazed.

"Now, come back up with me, you can't stand around like that in your underpants," said the girl.

Midge followed her to a lift. The door opened and they were whisked upwards.

"Um," he said pointing at her, "sorry, I can't remember your name?"

She raised her eyebrows.

"Lisa."

"Oh, Lisa, that's right. I had a skinful last night and my brain is just porridge this morning."

"Don't you remember last night, then?" she grinned.

"No, I don't," said Midge.

"Really? You don't remember?" she asked again.

Midge just shook his head.

Lisa puckered her lips and stayed silent. She still had a questioning look on her face.

"I think that you could do with some stim," she said, pulling him through the lift door into the living room. She opened the fridge door and did something. Midge didn't know what he was looking at.

"Here, get this down you," said Lisa, offering him a receptacle filled with brown liquid. It smelled like coffee, hot coffee. How did she get hot coffee from a fridge? He pointed at the fridge and decided not to ask the question.

Midge felt slightly better after the drink. It wasn't the coffee that he knew and loved, but it was okay.

Lisa came back into the living room with a pile of freshly laundered clothes. His clothes. They looked not only clean, but brand new. Again he repressed the question. He took the clothes from her and dressed. His mucky trainers looked new too. He just had to ask.

"How come my clothes and shoes look so new? What kind of washing machine have you got?"

She laughed. "Washing machine, what are you on about? I just got your clothes out of the re-cycler. They have been remanufactured using their original raw materials, what did you expect?"

Midge bit his lip.

Lisa was quite fanciable. She had a South London accent of sorts but no South London girl that he ever met had a pad like this.

"How can you afford all this?" he asked bluntly. "It must have cost a fortune."

Liza laughed out loud. "You must be kidding. It is just an ordinary council flat."

Midge gulped. This was certainly not his idea of a council flat.

"What do you do then, Lisa," he asked.

"Do? What do you mean 'do'?" she asked quizzically.

"Your job, what do you work at?" asked Midge.

She gave him one of those, 'are you mad?' looks.

"I don't work. Nobody works. Nobody has worked for years."

"How do you pay for things then?" asked Midge.

"Pay. I don't have to pay for anything. What a quaint, old fashioned idea."

Midge was getting to like this place. Wherever it was. Wandsworth? No way.

"I'm sorry, Lisa. You must think I'm a bit odd asking all these questions?"

"You seemed perfectly normal when I met you last night at the Chronos Club," said Lisa. "I'm not so sure now."

"Lisa, can I have another of those drinks. Maybe I can shake-off this memory lapse."

Lisa brought him another hot drink from the fridge. They sat down on the sofa together.

Liza ran a finger over Midge's thigh.

"You really don't remember last night," she asked with a playful smile.

"No, not a thing," said Midge in a matter of fact fashion.

"I won't forget it in a hurry," she said sidling closer.

Midge backed-off.

"How about we go out for a walk down to the river?" she asked. "It's nice down there."

The River Thames looked much the same as he remembered it. Some things never change. He did not remember the bridges that spanned it nor any of the tall buildings on either side. He tried not to look surprised.

A green park by the river held a children's playground. Parents sat watching their little ones yelling and having fun.

"What is this place?" he asked.

"Wandle Park," she replied. "Surely you must know Wandle Park. Don't you come from round here?"

"Yes, err, no," he answered, without elaborating.

"How about going for a drink," she suggested.

Even in a hungover state, Midge never refused a drink. It just wasn't him.

Lisa took him to a top floor bar in one of the swanky buildings opposite. The barman was a robot. A bolted to the ground robot. Midge tried not to react with terror. There were no bottles on shelves behind the bar. There were no colourful pump handles.

"What would you like?" asked Lisa.

"No, let me get this," said Midge, fumbling for his wallet.

"What are you talking about?" demanded Lisa.

"I'll get this round," said Midge.

"Don't be stupid," she said. "I told you already, we don't pay for anything."

"Oh, right," said Midge, pushing his wallet back into his inside pocket.

"What are you having?" she asked again.

"Err, pint of Special," he replied, but with a hint of a question on his face.

Lisa laughed.

"Pint? Of Special? We'll we don't use pints in Wandsworth these days. If I remember, it was quite a large measure of liquid a few hundred years ago. And Special. That comes in shot glasses but you don't want to hit that stuff this early in the day. It's only lunch time."

"Lunch?"

Midge remembered that he was hungry.

"Oh, let's have lunch then, but it's on me." Midge reached back for his wallet. Lisa shook her head.

"What did I tell you?"

They took a seat at a table with a wonderful view out over the river. Lisa had already ordered from the barman and another robot appeared with a tray of food and drinks. Midge didn't know what the food was. He would normally have had a burger and chips, and that's what he asked for. If these were chips, they were perfect cylinders. The burger was too. A layered cylinder. The side salad was a greenish colour but he didn't see any lettuce. It tasted a bit strange, but edible.

The small drinks seemed a bit sissy to him. He sipped one expecting it to taste like lager. Nothing like! Being a South London lad, he didn't drink cocktails. This was, in his opinion, a cocktail. Just as well that none of his mates were around.

Midge had no idea what he had just consumed but the fact that it was entirely free removed any questions from his mind.

"Shall we go for a bus ride?" asked Lisa.

"Yes, that would be nice," smiled Midge.

Instead of descending to the ground floor, the lift went upwards. They stepped out onto a rooftop helipad.

"That's funny, I remember there being a helipad around here," said Midge. "But it was down by the river."

"Helipad?" squinted Lisa. "This is a bus stop."

Just then, a large red quadcopter landed in front of them. "London Transport" it said on the side, along with a large yellow number '44'.

The doors opened. Midge was expecting to see a robot driver sitting at the front but there was no sign of any driver.

"Where are you thinking of going?" asked Midge.

"I was thinking the seaside would be nice."

"What, Brighton?" asked Midge. "The 44 doesn't go that far,"

"No, not Brighton, silly. Hawaii."

"Are you telling me that the 44 bus goes to Hawaii?"

"Oh, Midge. You haven't a clue, do you. We have to go to Victoria Hypergate Station first."

"Yes, of course," said Midge sheepishly.

"Hate these noisy things," said Lisa. "It's about time that London Transport bought some of the new hover craft."

"Hovercraft?" asked Midge. They are not very modern and they are very noisy."

"Hover craft float on anti-gravity drives. Totally silent. They have them in lots of cities all over the world. Here, they are just so far behind."

From the 'bus' window, Midge could see all the way to the horizon, and it was skyscrapers the all the way. One area had even taller spires and in a few places there were buildings that disappeared into the sky. He blinked.

Lisa pushed Midge towards the hypergate booth.

"We have to go separately," said Lisa. "Don't want to get our DNA scrambled. I don't mind getting down and dirty but that is just too intimate."

"How do I work it?" asked Midge. "Do I have to type-in a destination or something. I'm not very good at typing, or spelling."

"You just say where you want to go," said Lisa, beginning to show a degree of exasperation.

"What, just say Hawaii?" he asked.

"No, stupid, you have to be more specific than that. Say, 'Waikiki Beach, Honolulu."

"How long will it take?"

Another silly question! Lisa put her knuckles on her hips and scowled.

"It's instant. Are you really as dumb as you sound?" snarled Lisa.

Midge shrugged.

Lisa stepped into the hypergate booth. It was a little larger than a lift and surrounded by huge metallic coils. There was a flash like Midge would have expected in a photo booth. Lisa was gone.

What was this sorcery?

Midge stepped into the booth apprehensively and stated the destination.

"Waikiki Beach, Honolulu."

He expected to see a flash, but no, the wall in front of him simply dissolved like an image on a television screen. It became a beach scene – except that it wasn't a scene, it was a real beach shining in the moonlight. He felt dizzy and a little nauseous. Lisa was standing there waiting for him and took him by the hand.

"Look, isn't it lovely?"

Midge staggered. He had just travelled half way round the world in the blink of an eye. He felt like he had been given a good kicking. He had had a few of those in days gone by.

"It's the middle of the night?" he complained.

"Day, night. They are meaningless terms here," said Lisa, "It's a 24-hour resort. When you can drop-in from any time zone in the World for an hour or two, the only thing missing at night time is the sunburn."

People lay all over the beach in the moonlight. It was warm, comfortably so. Others splashed in the sea.

"It gets a bit hot in the daytime," explained Lisa. "I prefer the moonlight. Besides, it's more romantic."

She hooked her arm over his. They strolled around in the moonlight, had a couple of cocktails, and cuddled.

The silhouettes of coconut palms swayed on the soft night breeze. They found a holographic beach-bar. Midge was amazed at the cocktails appearing on the table in front of them out of thin air. He put his hand across the table and touched Lisa's fingers gently.

"Do you come here often?" he asked.

She smiled. "No, never been here in my life before. There are so many places to go, why go to the same place twice?"

That was a strange concept for Midge to grasp.

He usually went to the same place. The same place that he and his mates always went. It was on his way to 'The Goat' that he had noticed this new 'Chronos Club' and thought he would check it out.

Back on the 44 bus, Midge was thinking what a wonderful life this was. No need to work. Everything free. Luxury council flats. Day trips to Hawaii.

The best was yet to come.

"Feeling hungry?" asked Lisa.

The only negative aspects of hypergate travel, are the ways that it depletes the body's hydration and blood sugar. Lisa had insisted that he have a drink of isotonic water on their return to Victoria but Midge refused. It reminded him of sports. He was now both hungry and thirsty.

The robo-waiter took their orders and returned to their table within seconds. He had already requested the food from the central processor wirelessly and it was ready waiting for him when he reached the 'kitchen'. Midge didn't recognise much on the menu screen. He ordered 'steak and chips' but, by now, was prepared for something else. He was right. The tastefully arranged plate of food held neither steak nor chips on it. It wasn't even the cylindrical bars that he had a lunch time. This was more like the American interpretation of chips. He called them potato crisps. The steak was some sort of synthetic meat. Spun soya analogue was the term. It certainly tasted like steak. It had never been near an animal.

Midge had requested a long drink, he was thirsty.

There was nothing called beer or lager on the menu screen. He ordered something that sounded alcoholic. It was yet another bloody cocktail, but it had a kick and he liked it.

"Do you know what is in this drink?" he asked.

"Not exactly," said Lisa, "it's just another variety of synthohol. They are all the basically the same, only the colour and flavour are different."

"It still tastes quite powerful," said Midge, tapping the glass.

"Yes, but that is only an aspect of the flavour, the potency is the same as all other drinks. The buzz that it gives you only lasts a few hours and then goes."

"You mean, no hangovers?"

"I'm not entirely sure what you mean by 'hangover'. The buzz dissipates in two hours as I said. There are no ill effects after that."

*No hangovers*, thought Midge to himself. *I don't know if that is a plus or a minus.*

When they had finished their meals, the robo-waiter removed the empty dishes.

"Are we supposed to leave him a tip?" asked Midge.

"What's a tip?" asked Lisa.

"Oh, sorry. I forgot that you don't use money. I suppose that robots would have even less use for it."

"Oh, you mean a gratuity?" asked Lisa.

"Yes, that's what I was getting at. Tip. Gratuity. What's the difference?"

"Let me show you," said Lisa.

She beckoned the robot over. He bowed politely.

"You served us very well. Thank you very much."

The robot bowed even lower.

"There, the most valuable award for a robot is the honour of being treated like a human. They aspire to being considered equal. A simple thank-you and they are amply rewarded. To also be congratulated for their good service is their ultimate treasure."

Midge smirked. He had a lot of questions on the tip of his tongue but didn't relish the prospect of being called 'stupid' again. He kept quiet.

By now, the orange sun was setting on Wandsworth Town. He had already had an evening today and was just about to get another one. They took the lift to the sub-basement, jumped on a travellator, and in a few minutes were back at the building they started-off from.

"Do you realise that it took longer to cross the street than it did to go to Hawaii?" he observed.

"Someday soon, they will have hypergates in every building," she smiled.

"Yes, someone once predicted that, some day, there would be a telephone in every town," smiled Midge,

Lisa looked confused.

"What the heck is a telephone?" she inquired.

Back in Lisa's living room, Midge went over to the window. The city was ablaze with winking lights. He could see people moving about in the tower block opposite. Nobody seemed to care if they were being watched.

"Is there no privacy in these buildings?" he asked.

If you need privacy, you turn off the illumination."

"Oh."

"You will see soon," she smiled.

Lisa pointed at the wall. A huge 3D image appeared on it.

"Is that a television?" he asked.

"Television? What an interesting description. It's a vid. I think I like your word better though. Television. Yes, that sounds good."

Lisa ran her finger along the bottom of the screen and the channels changed. She ran it up the side and the volume increased.

"The off-world economy has increased by eight-percent in the last year. Asteroid mining shares have seen their greatest increase in five years. Meanwhile back in London, the weather bureau has set the temperature at twenty-one degrees for tomorrow and have deflected a group of rain clouds out over the bio-farms in Kent."

"Good Lord," thought Midge. "I can't ask Lisa about what I have just heard."

"Can I get you anything?" asked Lisa.

"No, I am fine at the minute," said Midge.

She went over to the fridge and produced two metallised receptacles.

"What's this?" he asked.

"Oh, you'll see," she answered.

Midge took a sip. It must have been some kind of synthohol, he thought. Whatever it was, it made him very relaxed in a matter of minutes.

Lisa did her thing with her finger along the bottom of the vid screen. The program changed to something like a screensaver. Soft music played. The room lighting decreased. She moved up close to him on the sofa.

"Midge," she whispered. "Do you really not remember what we did last night?"

Midge shook his head.

"I can't remember anything about last night," he said. "The night before perhaps. I was down the pub with my mates after work. I got a skinful of Special at The Goat. Perfectly ordinary night really, but I do remember some of it."

"Last night we came back here from The Chronos Club," said Lisa.

Midge shook his head.

"We sat here on the sofa and you put your arm round me."

"Really?" said Midge, a little embarrassed.

"Don't you remember what happened next?"

"No, I don't, I tell you, I remember nothing."

Lisa moved even closer to him and started to stroke his thigh. She put her lips up against his left ear and gave it a soft kiss. He was beginning to get the idea. He turned his head round and their lips met. They kissed a long lingering kiss.

"Just a minute, Midge," she said, diving back into the fridge. She came back with two more receptacles of liquid.

"Another cocktail?" he inquired.

"Something like that," she said provocatively.

Midge took a sip. It was not the same as the drink she had given him before.

"What is this?" he asked.

"Man power," she smiled. "Drink it all up, there's a good boy."

Midge did as he was told.

Lisa climbed up onto his lap, facing him. She kissed him some more. Her hand moved slowly down to his shirt buttons and undid them one by one. She pulled his shirt open and sunk her head into his chest, kissing it softly. She moved her hands inside his shirt and round to his back and hugged him tightly. Then, she jumped-up and nodded her head toward the bedroom. She pulled him up off the sofa and took him by the hand into her boudoir.

By this time, Midge was feeling very relaxed, and aroused too. He pushed her down onto the bed.

"Aren't we going to pull the curtains?" he asked.

"Curtains, what are curtains?" she grinned. "Oh, you are talking about privacy?" she asked. "Doesn't bother me but if it makes you more comfortable..." She pointed at the window and it changed from clear to smoked glass.

Silhouetted against the darkened window, Midge saw Lisa removing her clothes. She had a great figure. He took his off too, got up and held her tightly, skin to naked skin. They were near the window and it was still partly transparent – but what the hell, if she didn't care why should he.

All of a sudden, he began to feel very strange. It was a feeling of utter relaxation and euphoria at the same time. The two collapsed onto the bed. Midge felt like he was in a daze, a wonderful daze. An indescribably wonderful daze. The thought crossed his mind that she had given him some high-inducing potion. Was that what the last drink was? 'Man power,' she called it. He didn't care. Lisa did things to him that no girl had ever done before. He gasped in ecstasy.

They writhed together in the bed for an eternity.

"So, are you still saying that you don't remember last night," she whispered.

Mitch tried to shake his head but he didn't know if his head was moving or not. He was in a state of paralysed, blissful delirium.

"Ohhh…"

As his consciousness faded to blackness, Mitch came to the realisation that he had never made love with such intensely before. Who was this Lisa? Could he stay with her forever? He was wholly exhausted and floating around somewhere on a cloud. Lisa was at his side with her arms around him, purring deeply and blissfully.

When Midge woke-up, the first thing he noticed was that he was no longer lying on a warm comfy bed. He was in the cold, hard doorway of a boarded-up building. As he wiped the sleep from his eyes, he could see traffic going past. There was a Number

44 bus – with wheels. Just opposite was the familiar
'Goat' pub. He reached into his inside pocket
instinctively. Unlike the last time he had found
himself in this situation, his wallet was still there. But
wait, there was something else, something he didn't
recognise. It was a rectangle of a glass-like substance.
As he turned it over in his hand, it sprang into the air
in front of him and expanded out into a transparent
screen. It had lettering on it.

&lt;Hi Midge, I'm so sorry. I don't expect you to
understand what happened yesterday, I should have
realised. There was a timeslip at the Chronos Club
and... Anyway, thank you for a very wonderful day,
I'll miss you. Lisa xxx&gt;

Midge put out his hand to touch the screen
but there was nothing there. He shook his head in
bewilderment. As he stepped out into the High Street,
the letters briefly played across his face.

# The Daarnt

The Daarnt hadn't even seen a robot before, never mind tasted one.

It had always lived on the large asteroid, its diet gleaned from the sparse mineral deposits veining the surface. For an occasional treat, it would sometimes savour a mineral rich meteorite that would tumble in from the depths of space and rapidly be absorbed into the mass of its amorphous hydro-silicon body.

But here was a delicacy beyond its wildest dreams.

Struggling to escape the outer ripples of the viscous liquid body, the normally agile survey droid became firmly entrenched. Traction motors overloaded. Circuit breakers tripped. The power failed.

As the Daarnt slithered over the robot, it could, for the first time, taste delectable refined metals, exquisite alloys and sumptuous stainless steel. It slithered over the machine with ecstatic anticipation, oozing through nooks and crannies in the superstructure with consummate ease, exploring its catch with delight.

It went crazy with excitement.

Inside, it could sense an abundance of good things: metals, silicon of absolute purity, polycarbonates – they were less interesting – but wait, there, deep in the middle, was something special, something that smelled indescribably delicious.

As it drooled its gastric acids over the casing of the robot, an unheard distress signal was cut short. The long spiralling directional antenna dissolved into the bilious green pool. The outer panels succumbed to the onslaught of the corrosive juices as the Daarnt writhed in euphoria – never had there been a meal like this!

Through the holes in the collapsing skeletal remains, the Daarnt reached the electronics. Gold-plated copper was lapped from the circuit boards, tantalum gleaned from the capacitors, carbon from the resistors and oh, how it loved those sweet morsels of bright hard gold on the edge connectors.

As it devoured the outer resins of the logic chips, it found silver and other rarer metals.

What a meal!

When it reached the drive system, it quaffed a refreshing cocktail of lubricants and hydraulic fluid -missing only that which had spumed-out into the zero gravity vacuum under intense internal pressure.

The motors were greedily stripped of their copper field coils and soft iron armatures and disintegrated back into the quagmire. The stainless steel sub-frame bubbled as the corrosive liquids reacted with ferocity on the outer surface and eventually yielded. Beyond, was an exotic new metal, untried and intoxicating in its very promise. It would be reached soon, only the heavy metal shell had to be breached. The Daarnt quivered in anticipation, teasing itself by repeatedly touching the container and drawing back its tongues of green slime.

The temptation was overpowering. At last, with an eager gush it enveloped the shell and gnawed deep into the casing. As the metal gave way, it seeped through the first expanding cavity and touched the raw Plutonium.

For perhaps a microsecond, it experienced the most wonderful taste in the universe.

# A Digital Romance

"Haven't you finished yet?"

Alan Walker looked up from his microscope and rubbed his eyes.

"Won't be long, honey, just a few more to go."

Helen put her arm around him.

"You're overdoing it you know; you have to rest sometime."

Alan turned and kissed her lightly on the ear lobe.

"There'll be plenty of time for rest when we go Earthside next week," he said, putting another slide in the microscope and turning the focusing knob back and forth.

Helen flicked her short brown hair to the side and spun round on one foot in a joyful pirouette.

"Oh, I'm really looking forward to some fresh sea air."

She breathed deeply, almost smelling the salt and seaweed.

"After three months up in this sardine can, you really miss the simple things."

Walking over to the lab window, Helen looked out over the starry vista. She gazed longingly at the huge blue crescent as it came into view and slid silently across the sky.

Alan made a few hasty notes on a pad and closed it. He put a rack of micro-slides into a cabinet drawer and pulled a soft plastic cover over the microscope.

"I need a drink," he smiled wearily.

"Come on," said Helen, half pulling him out of the chair. "I've got a bottle of wine in the chiller. Let's celebrate."

"Celebrate what?" Alan asked, as if trying to remember some important event.

"Going home," laughed Helen.

"Oh. Yes!"


As the tired young biologist and his pretty white coated assistant closed the lab door, two small robots rolled down the corridor past them.

"Alan."

Helen tugged at his sleeve.

"Have you noticed how those two droids always seem to be doing the same job recently?"

He looked back as they disappeared into the bio lab.

"Yes, now you come to mention it, I have seen them together, but it hadn't occurred to me that there was anything particularly sinister. Do you think they are plotting a revolution or something? Going to take over the Starlab and hold us all to ransom?"

Helen gave him a playful shove.

"No, silly. I just don't see why it takes two droids to do a simple mop up job. It's not as if they are exactly overworked!"

"Yes, it does seem a bit pointless," said Alan, opening the door of the rest lounge.

"I'll check it out with Pete in the morning."


"Now I'm no expert," said Alan scanning the diagnostic report, "but these figures look pretty normal to me."

A tall spectacled man took the printout from his hand.

"I've run every test in the book on both of them and they are as clean as a whistle."

Pete Avery slapped the sheaf of papers with the back of his hand and peered over the top of his glasses.

"No, I don't think we need worry too much about having our throats cut in the middle of the night and waking up dead."

Helen grinned.

"But why are they always together?"

"Well," said Alan, looking deep into her eyes, "maybe they are in love..."

He pulled her close but she backed off irritably, taking the sheets of folded paper from Pete and glancing at the top line.

"I suppose it has escaped your attention that they are close relatives," she inquired.

The two men looked at her in puzzlement.

"Look at their serial numbers, UR109307, UR109308. They are consecutive."

"Ok, so that's a coincidence, but it doesn't explain this behaviour," Alan snapped.

Helen put her hand at the back of his neck and scratched him softly behind the ear.

"I know," she said winking at Pete. "It shouldn't make any difference."

Alan tapped a few keys on the terminal.

"Look, I tell you what. I'll give them specific jobs to do at opposite ends of the station."

Pete stood and watched as Alan altered some code on the screen. When Alan became stuck, Pete would reach over and add a line here and there. Alan nodded in appreciation.

Ten minutes later, the two droids trundled out of the workshop and headed in opposite directions.

"It's really weird," said Alan. "There are ... what ... eighteen droids on this platform and sixteen of them give no trouble at all, but Tom and Jerry here have to start acting up."

Helen took him by the arm and led him out.

"Thanks Pete."


"So where are you off to next week?"

Michael Fisher leaned back in his big chair and clasped his hands together.

Alan relaxed.

"Helen and I are going to Coral Beach for a few days to get some real sun."

The burly man leaned forward across the desk.

"You and Helen. Don't you see enough of her up here?"

Alan blushed slightly and moved uneasily in his chair.

"I see, it's like that is it?" smiled the director. "That reminds me, Pete Avery said something about trouble with the droids. I wasn't really paying much attention. It's funny because I was just over at the transmat half an hour ago and overheard one of the girls saying that she had seen what she described as 'Frankie and Johnny' loading trash into the vaporiser.

It didn't click at the time..."

"But I reprogrammed them a couple of days ago," chimed in Alan. "It can't be possible."

He got up and headed for the door.

"Have a nice time," called Fisher.

"What?", said Alan, hesitating.

"At Coral Beach."

"Oh yes," muttered Alan, his mind in another direction completely.

"I just don't get it."

Alan paced the length of the workshop and back to where Pete was standing.

"I reprogrammed those droids and still they came back together."

"No," interrupted Pete. "Your manual over-ride was only temporary. As soon as they carried out your specific instructions, they dropped back into firmware."

"You mean they reverted to a basic maintenance program", Alan quizzed, "but surely all the droids would run around together, aren't their programs identical?"

"Up to a point," answered the electronics engineer, "but they do have differences, otherwise they would, as you say, all do the same thing all the time."

"So that's what it is, these two just have the same program somehow," said Alan with a relieved sigh.

Pete shook his head.

"I've already checked that. They are totally

different, 307 should not be on this level at all, it should be down on deck three, in stores."

Helen backed away from the window.

"Geostationary orbit is so boring; you always get the same view."

She climbed up on to a workbench and swung her legs back and forth.

"Why don't you forget about this droid thing, isn't it getting out of all proportion?" she asked.

Alan got agitated.

"Look, even Fisher was talking about it, and other people have noticed too."

Pete joined in with a shrug.

"So they've got the hots for each other..."

Helen eyes went up to the ceiling and she groaned. She swung herself back down on to the floor and grabbed Alan's arm.

"Hey, we are booked-in for squash at three, remember?"

She pulled him in the direction of the door.

"Yes I know," Alan replied. "Look, you go on down and I'll catch up with you in five minutes. There's something I have to do."

The door hissed open and Helen bounced out.

"Hurry up, it's nearly three now," she called back as the door slid back.

"Pete, can I borrow your toolkit?" asked Alan.

"What do you want it for?" said Pete with a puzzled expression.

"I just want to try something," came the reply.

"Hey, you're not going to start messing around with

those droids are you. You don't know what you are doing."

Alan looked at the floor.

"Uh ... oh no, nothing like that. I've, er, I've got to open up the separator. Something's fallen down the inside and it squeaks like hell. I'll bring it back in an hour, ok?"

"I thought you were playing squash with Helen," Pete mused.

"Yes, you're right. Can we make it two?"

"Go on, but remember what I said, no messing with the droids."

Helen was busy knocking the ball against the wall when Alan came in.

"You took your time, our court time's half over," she complained.

Alan stepped in and took over from her rhythmic volleys.

"I don't suppose I should really tell you this," she said, "but I've just seen your two friends down the corridor."

Alan missed the ball.

"They shouldn't be on this level should they?" she continued.

He thought for a moment.

"Well, one of them is assigned to stores, but the other belongs up top in the lab section."

A few half-hearted swipes later he turned to Helen.

"Look, Helen, I'm not really in the mood for this,

what do you say we meet up later?"

"Oh, come on, just a quick match," she insisted, jumping up and down with seemingly boundless energy.

"We'll play some real squash when we get down to Coral Beach, I can't handle this low-G stuff and curved floor, it puts me off."

Alan pecked her on the cheek and slung his holdall over his shoulder.

"See you later."

The narrow beam from an LED torch lit the inside of the droid. A cluster of ribbon cable arched out of the carcass and into the output port of Alan's terminal.

"That will sort you out, you little sod," Alan smirked. "Let me see you get out of that one."

The door opened.

"What the hell are you doing?" came Helen's voice. "You shouldn't be ... if somebody finds out, you'll be in big trouble."

Alan swivelled round on his chair.

For a moment he looked at her in the way that a boss would look at an erring subordinate.

"Helen, there's something wrong with one, or both of these droids. They are running around like together for no good reason and I've just got to get to the bottom of it."

"If the company finds out you are tampering with their robots, you'll be for the high jump," she said sternly. "Besides, you'll get Pete into trouble too.

They are his responsibility."

As if on cue, Pete walked in.

"Just as I thought. I just put a trace on these two and there was no reply. I figured that you might be behind it."

Alan unplugged the connectors and shut the access panel like a naughty child just caught raiding the fridge.

"I was just checking their hardware. You're right. They are different."

"The hell you were," stormed Pete. "You were trying to overwrite the firmware. You fool, you can't do that without special equipment, even I can't do that up here."

Helen joined the fray.

"I'm sure he was just looking," she said, trying desperately to cover up for her companion. "Look, the droids are fine, they are going back to work..."

"What did you do?"

Helen cuddled up beside Alan on the couch in front of the video screen.

"Nothing, really," he said, putting his arm around her.

John Wayne leaned out of the stage-coach window and picked-off another stuntman that was trying to uncouple the horses. The twenty-first shell from his six shooter had found its target. A painted warrior fell between the horses, hung on for a few seconds, and went on to the happy hunting ground.

"Bitter aloes," said Alan cryptically.

"What?" said Helen sitting up.

"Didn't you ever bite your nails?"

Alan took her by the back of the neck and squeezed gently.

"Aversion therapy," he giggled. "I've programmed them to hate each other, that should keep them apart..."

They waited by the docking bay airlock.

The not-so-slim silhouette of Michael Fisher entered the departure room.

"Ah, you're off, I see," he smirked. "Off for a week of sin and sand?"

Helen couldn't stand the man. How did he ever become director of a space platform? It certainly wasn't through tact.

"Got your bikini packed then?" he said with a sleazy look in his piggy eyes.

"Hey, did you hear about those two droids?"

The change of subject caught Helen unawares.

"The droids?"

"Yes, those two droids that were running around together, you know, Romeo and Juliet, or whatever they were calling them today. It seems that they went into the garbage transmat and fired it up remotely, I mean, they are like space dust. Kaput! Beamed out into deep space on maximum dispersion. Christ, why would they do such a thing? They cost half a million bucks each. What do I tell the board?"

The shuttle fell away from the space station on the

end of a plume of blue thrust jets. Helen's slim hand held on to Alan. Earthfall was an experience that was not new to either of them, but it still had its terrors. Somehow space had become their home. The lower gravity. The smell of the recycled air. The acceptance of the microcosm of a half-mile wide wheel spinning in the eternity of space. Its vulnerability, its all-or-nothingness.

"You know that they had consecutive serial numbers?" Helen half whispered.

Alan looked back from the window and nodded.

"Does that mean they were ... like brother and sister?" she said.

"Don't be crazy," Alan barked. "They were only droids."

"But you tampered with their programming. That can be the only explanation..."

The shuttle bucked as it hit the first wisps of the Earth's outer atmosphere. Helen's hand tightened its grip on his.

"... Or maybe ..."

Alan gazed into her soft brown eyes as she spoke.

"Haven't you ever heard of Lover's Leap?"

**G**

A light breeze brushed past the robot's face on the delightfully sunny, summer's day. Fluffy white clouds hung motionless in the sky above, but this particular robot had other things on his mind. His main concern, at this instant, on such an idyllic day, was the fact that the Earth was rushing up to meet him at a rather alarming rate.

The Universal Robotics Autotropic UR103 was capable of calculations to an incredible 512 decimal places of accuracy. Its sensors told it that, at this moment in time, it was exactly 400 metres from the ground. The calculation took less than a millionth part of a nanosecond. What the robot's totally unsurpassed silicon brain could not comprehend was why it had been ordered to step out of the plane in the first place!

```
<<< Altitude 400 metres >>>
```

The robot scanned its memory banks for an appropriate phrase.

"Ours is not to reason why, ours it is to do or..."

For the first time, the idea occurred to the 2.5503657-metre-high metal man, that there might be something potentially terminal about its current situation and so, reserved a small part of its gargantuan mental capacity to work on the problem.

**Fact One.**

It was an Orion UR103, the most advanced piece of cybernetic hardware ever built.

**Fact Two.**

It had mental reasoning powers beyond that of any other mobile computer system.

**Fact Three.**

It had instant remote network access to the largest computer databases in the world.

**Fact Four.**

It was advertised in a glossy promo video as being 'totally indestructible'.

**Fact Five.**

It was 200 metres from the ground. And falling fast.

```
<<< Altitude 200 metres >>>
```

The robot considered the facts in logical sequence.

Yes. It was one of the most advanced robots ever built. It actually felt pride, that's how advanced it was!

Its computing power was awesome, but it took that for granted.

It could draw on the sum total of man's experience in microseconds over its telemetry link-up and that was in itself of some comfort.

Ah. It was indestructible. Now that was particularly interesting. What that meant, outside the advertising hype, was that its polymer-alloy frame could absorb any physical shock and simply convert the kinetic energy into stored electricity.

So...

Indestructible!

It may have been created by man in his own image, but some attention to practicalities had been given to the design. It was essentially immortal.

On checking out 'indestructible' in its thesaurus database, the UR103 encountered various synonyms. When it came to 'unsinkable' it paused. Wasn't the Titanic 'unsinkable'?

The robot laser-triangulated its distance from the ground: 105.46284 metres. It thought that it might be a good idea to devote some more of its computing capacity to the problem in hand. Another part of its brain was still trying to work out why it was in the predicament.

```
<<< Altitude 100 metres >>>
```

Now, brain power alone is insufficient to alter the rate of descent of 500 odd kilos of mechanical man but, nevertheless, the robot switched in more and more of its processing power until just under one metre from the ground it could summon no more.

Trillions of logic gates flipped and flopped and, amongst many other things, the robot worked out that its velocity would be more or less constant for the last metre of the journey. To travel half this distance would take 144 microseconds. To cover the next half of its journey would take 72 microseconds. To cover the next half of its journey would take 36 microseconds. It projected that it could, theoretically, halve the one metre (or slightly less now) an infinite number of times. As infinity can never be attained, it would never actually reach the ground...

At one millimetre from the ground, the time taken to travel each successive half distance was becoming increasingly short and even the 512 decimal places of accuracy were being stretched to their limit.

```
<<< Altitude 1 millimetre >>>
```

Meanwhile, in a tiny corner of its brain, it was replaying the situation immediately prior to leaving the plane...

"It cost what?" exclaimed the security guard.

"The best part of half a billion," replied the technician, polishing the robot's platinum coloured forehead. "There has never been one like it."

"Yeah. It has a nice finish, but apart from that, it looks like a pretty ordinary droid to me," said the guard, testing the restraining straps.

"Don't you believe it," the tech insisted. "This is the ultimate mechanical man. Universal are going to clean up with this model."

"What time is the convention," asked the guard.

"Four. We will have to head straight there when we land," came the reply.

"Say, Buddy, any chance of a demonstration of this-here marvel of modern science?" whispered the uniformed man.

The tech looked around the cargo hold, to make sure they were alone.

"Well, I'm not supposed to give demonstrations but ... I guess it won't do any harm," said the tech reaching up to the robot's chest and opening a small door. Inside he pressed a green button. The robot twitched and came to life.

"Err... Hi there. Can you hear me?" asked the guard, standing on his toes and looking into the thing's eyes.

"Of course I can," the robot answered, with perfect articulation and no hint of synthesis.

The guard hesitated, then pointed.

"Hey. It's good. It's good." He smiled at the tech. "Can I try something?"

"Go ahead," said the other. "Ask it a question."

"OK. Who scored the winning pitch in the final of the '56 Indiana League, Big Boy?" quizzed the guard.

"Madison, M. The final score was 36-30. The game ended at fifteen thirty-two on the fourteenth of June at Reagan Stadium," came the reply.

The guard grinned at the tech.

"Jee-suz ... You're right there, Boy. I've never seen

a droid that could do that. Let me try another?"

The tech nodded.

"Do you know the exact whereabouts of Thelma Johnson. Age 32, blonde hair, blue eyes, height about four eleven. Comes from Portland, Oregon originally?" The guard winked at the smaller man.

"A Thelma Johnson, that fits your description, is currently residing at 1113, Lakeside Drive, Apartment 47, Toronto, Canada. She is a biochemist." stated the robot.

"No. Not my Thelma," laughed the guard. "She's no biochemist..."

"Wait," interrupted the robot. "There is another. At The Belleview Motel, 3638 Santa Monica Boulevard, Fairfax, California. She's with a man called Mendoza."

"What!!!" coughed the guard. "That little bitch. I just knew there was something going on..."

The tech pulled on his sleeve.

"Look. I could get in trouble for this, better stop now."

"No way. I want to know how long this has been going on," argued the guard. "This guy Mendoza is just a jerk."

The tech shook his head.

"This machine cost half a billion bucks, it's not some tin pot private eye..."

The guard pushed him back.

"Easy now. I think I'd better switch this thing off," said the tech reaching for the button.

The guard grabbed him by the neck and twisted his arm half way up his back. It hurt.

"Where does this guy Mendoza live, Robot. I'll kill the rat," fumed the guard.

The tech struggled.

"Over-ride code 45, don't tell him ... uh!" he shouted before the strong arm tightened around his neck.

"Where does Mendoza live?" the guard called breathlessly.

An orange light on the robot's control panel lit up.

"Restricted information," it replied.

The guard pushed the choking tech to floor and looked the robot straight in the eyes.

"Where does he work, you heap of scrap iron?

"Restricted information," echoed the robot.

The guard swiped angrily at the robot's chest, inadvertently punching a cluster of buttons in the process.

"Oh, go take a hike..."

```
<<< Altitude 0.001 millimetre >>>
```

So, one thousandth of a millimetre from the ground, the robot still did not know why it was there, but was content in the knowledge that it had three very good reasons why it would come to no harm whatsoever.

**A.**

Men would not allow anything potentially damaging to happen to such a unique and expensive piece of equipment...

**B.**

It was totally indestructible and...

**C.**

It would never actually reach the ground anyway...

Mother Earth disagreed entirely.

# In the White Room

The baby cried.

Babies do.

Crying can have so many interpretations. A mother will usually come to understand what those cries mean and respond to them appropriately.

Sometimes not.

He could have been hungry, or uncomfortable. Maybe he was just seeking attention. He certainly wasn't cold, even though he was completely naked. The ambient temperature was just perfect for a tiny human.

The little boy had a wisp of black hair on top and was neither too skinny nor too plump.

Perfectly proportioned.

His skin colour was fairly average too – a healthy shade of café au lait with no blemishes nor distinguishing marks of any kind.

A slight rocking motion began. The crying gradually faded-off into a soft gurgle.

Eyes closed.

Slumber.

His little chest moved up and down slowly as he breathed.

The featureless white room was bathed in a soft, yellow light. The air was pure, and still. There was no sound at all, only the very faintest vibration from a filter motor somewhere.

The crib was a white, smooth memory-foam mattress that gave ever so slightly with the baby's weight. The small indentation in the mattress and its rigid edges formed a nest that kept him solidly in place.

Time passed, slowly and peacefully.

The baby's eyes opened. His mouth opened too and, as if someone had released a pause button, the crying continued from where it had left off before, but now with more veracity and urgency.

With a soft whirr, a transparent tube dropped down from above and arrived at his mouth. After a moment of hunting, he wrapped his lips around the soft teat and began to suck vigorously. A milky, green liquid flowed down the tube bringing contentment and nourishment.

Patterns of pastel-coloured lights played on the ceiling.

He could see the movement and held out his hands towards them, but there was nothing to touch. This nursery mobile is but a trick of light.

Baby's eyes widened and lips puckered. His little body stiffened. Could it be…?

Yes.

Splat!

As there was nothing to catch it, the mess went all over the nest – and was followed quickly by an arc of pale yellow liquid high into the air.

A nozzle descended from the ceiling and sprayed white foam around the baby's bottom and out to the extent of his spray. The foam bubbled, turned beige, then white again – and dissolved into nothing at all.

A second nozzle sprayed a fragrant, disinfecting fine mist where the mess had been. A stream of warm air wafted across bringing a delighted "cooo" from the little one.

His thumb went into his mouth and his eyes closed again.

We'll call him 'Josh', although he doesn't actually have a name. He does have an identity, but it is long, not very memorable and more in keeping with a product serial number than a birth certificate.
Josh is very well looked after. His every need is catered for but Josh has never, in his short life, seen another human nor has any concept of what he is. He just IS.

As the months go by, Josh grows and becomes more mobile. He is able to roll over onto his tummy and propel himself to the edge of his cot. He tumbles off onto a soft floor and cries. This is a strange place. This is not his place. He cries and cries and falls asleep. When he awakens, he finds that he is back in his place. The tube comes down from above and he drinks greedily.

The baby is fascinated by this new 'not his place' beside his bed. He tumbles out deliberately. On the floor, he rolls over onto all fours and finds that he can crawl. Apart from the slightly raised dais that is his bed, the room is featureless. There is nothing else to catch his attention. He heads for the bed and puts his hands on it. Pushing with all his might, he is able to get his elbows up onto the bed and is mostly supported by his short, rubbery legs.

One week and many similar excursions later, Josh finds that he can stand unsteadily. He tries taking his hands off the bed and sits down abruptly as he loses his balance. The soft floor mercifully cushions his fall. He tries again and again and, in a short time, he is able to make his way round the room.

From his new standing viewpoint, he notices for the first time that there is a bump on the wall that is not white like everything else. He makes his way over to it and looks at it curiously. This is different, interesting. He touches it and is startled by the beep and change of colour. He cries and waddles back to the comfort of his familiar bed place. He glances back at the hemispherical bump on the wall suspiciously. It is pale again and is not making any sound. He plucks up the courage to try this again. Yes, it was frightening, but it was also interesting.

Gingerly, he touches the bump again. Sure enough, it makes a beeping sound and changes colour. Josh is shocked but manages not to cry. Apart from the greenish tint of his food and the patterns on the ceiling, he has not experienced bright colour. What is it? What does it mean?

After a sleep, Josh notices that there are now two bumps, one beside the other. There was only one before. Why? He moves over and touches the second bump. It makes a clicking sound and lights-up in a different colour. It is bright and alluring. He touches the first bump again and then the second. They are not the same. One beeps, the other clicks, and they are different colours.

He alternates between the two bumps with his two hands and is joyous in his discovery. He has no words for the colours or the sounds, but he recognises them and differentiates between them.

A few sleeps later, Josh notices that the bumps are no longer pale. They are now strongly coloured – the same colours that they used to be after he touched them. This has to be investigated. He crawls over to the wall with the bumps and stands-up on his legs. He touches one bump, the one that beeped. It beeped. It did something else, it got even brighter.

He tried the other one. It clicked and got brighter. This was odd. He decided to push both at the same time. Something strange and frightening happened. A hole in the wall opened and a shelf slid out.

He was very worried. When he composed himself, he examined the shelf. It had a small, round, flat object on it. He took it with his hand and examined it closely. As babies do, he put it in his mouth. It had a taste. His usual tube-delivered meals had a taste but this was different. He liked it. He kept it in his mouth and the hard object gradually softened and he swallowed it. By now, the opening in the wall had disappeared. He touched a bump with his hand and, as before, it lit up but there was no shelf. He pushed both bumps together – beep, click – the shelf slid out with another morsel. He put it in his mouth immediately and drooled.

Over the next few days, Josh continually helped himself to the food. He now knew that he had to push the two bumps at the same time to get the drawer to come out. Neither bump did anything on its own. Then he discovered that a third bump had appeared. He touched it and there was a little 'ting' sound and it lit-up in a new colour. Apart from that, it did nothing. He then remembered that he had to touch two bumps for anything to happen, so he touched the new bump with one hand and one of the others with the other.

The tray slid out but there was something different on it. Not the little round disc but something spherical and transparent. He immediately put it into his mouth. It had no taste at all. The disc had a delicious taste, why didn't this? He bit it with his gums. It burst and flooded his mouth with a wonderful-tasting liquid. The liquid seeped from the edges of his tiny mouth and ran down his chin. This was good. Very good.

Josh experimented with the three bumps. Pressing the original two at once gave him the disc, another two gave him the liquid sphere. Pressing the third combination gave him a little cube made from a soft, yellow squidgy substance. He didn't call it yellow or sweet, but it was, and he liked it. Now he had three choices, all equally good. Josh would have gorged on the foodstuff until he burst but he found that after a while, the bumps stopped working. No amount of coaxing would make the little tray come out.

After a sleep, he was delighted to find that his bumps worked again. The food tube no longer came down from the ceiling.

As time passed, the number of bumps on the wall increased. There were now as many bumps as he had fingers on one hand. One of the new bumps was larger than the other four. He now found that pressing two bumps would only open the hole in the wall – the tray didn't come out with the food. What was wrong?

It was only by sheer persistence and determination that he discovered that he had to press the larger bump to make the tray come fully out and deliver the contents. He had to push two bumps to make the door open and the large bump to extend the tray. He also found that different combinations of the four smaller bumps delivered other foods and drinks when followed by a large bump press. There were two liquid bubbles, one clear, one white. There was a disc, a cube, a triangle and an amorphous blob. The triangle was wonderful, his favourite taste of all. After tasting the blob, he ejected it with his tongue and spat it onto the floor. It was disgusting. An arm swung down from above and sprayed the mess on the floor and it dissolved in a white foam, as it always did.

Josh was growing. His legs were becoming sturdier and he sprouted baby teeth. He could toddle round the white room and feed himself at will. He did like those triangles but he never summoned-up the blobby stuff again. He learned to avoid that combination.

When the fifth small bump appeared, Josh was quite excited. He now had three liquid bubbles to choose from and seven solid foodstuffs – well, six if he ignored the horrible blobby stuff. The two new food shapes were a cylinder with rounded ends and a hemisphere. Intriguingly, the hemispheres arrived in different colours at random. Each colour had a different taste. They were all good but he liked the red ones best, they were sweet and juicy. The yellow one was a little too tart for his taste, although he didn't spit it out.

The other strange thing that Josh just noticed was that the morphing colours on the ceiling were beginning to take distinct shapes. He recognised the shapes and colours of his food. He giggled and held his arm outstretched at the ceiling.

"Coo," he said.

The triangular shape flashed and spun round.

"Oooh."

He waved his little hand at the ceiling. The triangle matched his hand movements but he didn't notice at first. There was so much going on up there. All of the other shapes faded leaving just the triangle, which had stopped spinning. As Josh moved his arm, the triangular shape on the ceiling matched his arm movements perfectly. He moved it from side to side. The triangle followed. He moved it up and down and the triangle moved back and forward. He waved his arm in a big circle. The triangle described the same motion.

Josh smiled. He had a toy.

Josh soon realised that if he pointed at a food shape on the ceiling, it flashed and he could move it around by moving his arm. He began to give the shapes names.

The round one was "Bee". That was as near as he could get to "beep".

"Kaa," he said, pointing at the triangle.

"Googoo," was the square.

The name for the clear liquid bubble was vocalised with a click of his tongue and the white liquid, a sort of slushy sound.

He didn't give the amorphous blob a name, he just pulled a face.

Over the next few sleeps, he reminded himself of the food names, then something strange happened. He moved "Kaa" across the ceiling and onto the wall that held the dispenser. The tray slid out with a "Kaa" on it. He liked "Kaa", and took it.

He then tried the same with "click" and was rewarded with a clear bubble of liquid. He crushed it with his baby teeth and drank the contents.

The next time he looked at the dispenser place, the bumps had disappeared. He just had to check that moving the food shapes over to the wall with his arm still worked. Yes, the dispensing tray produced the food shape he had chosen.

Josh felt happy, gurgled, and did a roll onto his low bed. Everything he wanted was available with a wave of his hand! He could even amuse himself by flicking the food shapes across the ceiling into one another and see them bounce around like billiard balls. Sometimes a shape would hit the dispenser wall and the tray would open accidentally with the appropriate titbit. If he didn't get to the tray quickly enough, it would close and take the food back with it.

Happy as he was, he felt that there was something wrong. He didn't know quite what it was, but something was missing.

Josh had dreams. He would roll around his bed in his sleep and his eyes moved behind his eyelids. He even waved his arms in his sleep, summonsing-up unheard of delicacies perhaps? There is no way of telling.

Not long after waking, he would peer-up at the ceiling and the shapes immediately reminded him of food. Lovely food.

He would say "Kaa", and fling the triangle across at the dispenser wall. He could roll out of bed and walk straight and steadily to the dispenser, grab the food and toss it into his mouth – but this time there was a problem. There was something between the triangle and the dispenser wall. Something that the triangle would not go through. It was a virtual wall. Josh pondered the situation. He had never encountered an obstacle anywhere. This line of light was blocking the path of the triangle to its target. He tried flicking the triangle against the obstacle more deliberately, but it simply rebounded.

Josh was beginning to feel frustration. He hadn't eaten for some time and was feeling hungry. The denial made him even hungrier. It was then that he noticed that the barrier did not stretch the full width of the ceiling, there was a gap at each end. One gap was quite narrow but the other one was wide enough … yes … He could move the shape over to the gap and bypass the barrier. Then, he flicked it against the dispenser wall and got his prize.

He felt so proud.

On waking from the next few sleeps, he discovered increasingly more barriers were blocking his food shapes from the dispenser wall. Each had a gap in it so he knew it was just a matter of manoeuvring the shape through the gaps to the walls. Eventually, the barriers became a maze. He had to go left and right, and sometimes backwards and forwards, to guide the symbol to its target. The symbols became smaller and the maze more complex. Sometimes it would take quite a while to navigate the maze – but he always got there eventually.

Josh actually enjoyed the puzzles, but the next one was more challenging. All the food shapes, except one, were boxed-off along the ceiling opposite the food-dispenser wall. The only shape that was free to be moved was the amorphous blob. He sat down hard with a frown on his face. He didn't want that stuff, it was horrible. He wasn't going to play this game.

Unfortunately, the game did not change. Even

after two sleeps, it was still the same. He was getting very hungry now. He started to move the shape towards the target wall but then stopped. He was determined not to complete the puzzle. He remembered the nasty taste in his mouth. He had tried dislodging the other shapes from their enclosures but that didn't work. He was so hungry. He decided to go for it. The blobby shape was taken through the maze to its destination, the tray opened and there is was in all its horror.

He gingerly lifted the food to his mouth and touched it with his tongue. It wasn't as bad as he had remembered. He put the food into his mouth and chewed slowly. It wasn't as pleasant as the other offerings, but he managed to eat it. After the next two sleeps, his maze only gave him the options of the blobby stuff or the clear bubble. He was still hungry so he didn't hesitate to access the food he didn't like so much.

One sleep later, all his options were back, plus a few new ones. One was a long orange conical shape and another, blunter, red cone. The red cone was really good and the orange one – mmm, okay.

The foodstuffs given to Josh were analogues. Nutritionally balanced lookalikes of real foods, but completely synthetic and concocted in a processing unit a metre behind the dispensing slot. It had to be like that!

Josh knew that by this time when the coloured shapes disappeared off the wall and the room became pure white, it was time to stand in the corner and have the lovely warm water sprayed over his body. There was a time when this happened when he was in his bed but the shower head gradually moved away from the bed into a corner and he followed it. He liked the shower. The water ran through tiny holes in the floor and in 30 seconds, the floor was totally dry again. He had also learned to use this corner as his toilet. The sweet smelling, white foam spray took care of the mess and the shower spray washed the foam away through the perforations in the floor.

Warm air caressed his small, but growing, body.

Josh was bright, but there were lots of things he didn't notice. He was totally oblivious, for instance, to the fact that his sleeps were of different lengths. As far as he was concerned, he felt sleepy, closed his eyes, fell asleep, maybe dreamed, and woke up. Every now and then, his sleep would be considerably longer. This was one of those sleeps.

Before he would go to sleep, a soft, barely perceptible sound filled the room – a lullaby. As the lullaby increased in volume from imperceptible to only just audible, his eyelids would flicker and droop and he would slip into deep slumber. The lighting would dim.

As he slept this deeper sleep, strange machines emerged from a concealed panel in the wall. They were propelled on either rubber tracks or soft, balloon wheels. They sprouted multiple arms ending in soft pads and an assortment of forceps, needles and instruments of unimaginable purpose. They lifted him, weighed him, scanned him, took blood samples and various physical measurements and laid him back, ever so gently, on his bed.

He slept on.

The medi-droids disappeared back into the wall and were gone.

The lullaby faded back to silence. The lights brightened. He awoke with a start. He had had a dream, and it bothered him. After a few minutes, all memories of the dream had faded and he started playing with the food shapes on the ceiling.

Now there were many more food shapes. Some he recognised and some he didn't. He found that now, he could flick several symbols against the dispenser wall and the selections would appear together in the tray. Sometimes there would be a puzzle to solve but not immediately after a sleep. Puzzles were for later when he was fully awakened. Josh didn't know what an important day this was going to be.

The first thing he noticed was a sound. Where his lullaby was subliminal, this sound was slightly louder. It raised and lowered in pitch in an intriguing pattern. It was music. Josh opened his mouth in wonder and looked all around the room to see what was causing it. He couldn't see anything but it sounded good. It made him feel happy.

Josh smiled a big smile and tried to mimic the sounds with his mouth.

ANNUAL DEVELOPMENT REPORT SUMMARY

SUBJECT: JSH-19102052/017

REPORT DATE: 19/10/2053

AGE: 1 YEAR EXACTLY

WEIGHT: 10.4kg

HEIGHT: 78.2cm

HEAD CIRCUMFERENCE: 47.1cm

BMI: AGA

FOOD INTAKE: NORMAL

FLUID INTAKE: NORMAL

SLEEP PATTERNS: NORMAL

EYESIGHT: EXCELLENT

HEARING: EXCELLENT

CURIOSITY: ABOVE AVERAGE

HAND/EYE COORDINATION: EXCELLENT

INTELLIGENCE: WELL ABOVE AVERAGE

BLOOD SUGAR: SLIGHTLY ELEVATED


COMMENTS: SUBJECT DEVELOPMENT NORMAL AND
SATISFACTORY. RECOMMEND CONTINUANCE.
MODIFY DIET. REDUCE SUGAR AND
CARBOHYDRATES. INCREASE PROTEIN AND FIBRE.


NEXT FULL TEST: 19/10/2054


FULL DEVELOPMENT CHARTS APPENDED

234

Josh had no idea that it was his first birthday, but it seemed like a special day. There was happy music. He decided it was time for some food. Something new amidst his food shapes on the ceiling was a spinning triangle with one curved edge. It was spinning in three dimensions showing that it was, in fact, a wedge shape. One end was white, the other a golden brown. In the middle was a pale yellow colour with a red line up the middle. It threw itself against the dispensary wall without any action from Josh. The tray opened. He waddled over. He took the small wedge from the tray and it slid closed. He licked the wedge. It was sweet and soft. He liked it and wanted some more but the symbol had now vanished from the ceiling.

He spotted another new symbol, quite unlike all the others. It hadn't been there before. It was an oval shape with a circle stuck-on at one end. There was a straight long shape on either side and two more at the opposite end from the circle. He flicked it against the dispensary wall but the tray didn't open. Instead, the entire wall lit-up. Strangely, it now looked as if his room had doubled in size. There was another bed in the distance but there in the middle was a boy. A boy just like him. It had a body, arms and legs and a head. Josh put out his hand towards the boy. It did the same to him. He walked towards it. The boy walked towards him. Josh put both hands out to touch the boy, the boy did the same. When the hands met, they were cold and hard.

Josh moved his head from side to side. The other

boy copied him. Every move that Josh made was aped. He went up close to the other boy and their lips met. The boy had no taste, it was just solidness. He backed-away from the wall and tumbled into his bed. The other boy did too. Everything that Josh did, the other boy copied.

Eventually, Josh came to the understanding that this other boy was, in fact, himself. He didn't understand it, but he accepted it. The image on the dispenser wall gradually faded away but the new boy-shape remained on the ceiling.

Between sleeps, Josh would often summons-up the other boy. He would try to outwit it, try to make a move that the other boy didn't or watch for a move that he didn't perform. He would hold out food to the other boy but it did the same, boringly and predictably. He put food into his mouth and chewed. He opened his mouth to show the food inside. The boy just did the same.

This was getting tedious.

Josh soon forgot about the other boy. He was no fun at all!

As the sleeps passed, Josh ate, slept and did puzzles. Often, new food shapes would appear on the ceiling and he would dutifully explore them – and the contents of the resulting tray from the dispensary. He noticed that some of the foods delivered had changed size. His favourite triangle was now smaller and the green, amorphous blob was bigger. He hadn't been able to compare the old and new directly – he was simply relating them to the size of his hand. When he tried to 'order' more triangles, the triangle symbol on the ceiling faded to grey and wouldn't work as expected. Instead of operating the dispensing tray, it appeared as a realistic image on the wall. Josh was confused. Symbols appeared beneath the image of the brown triangular foodstuff.

<C ... H ... O ... C>

This was accompanied by a sound. A sound that Josh recognised as a mouth sound.

"Choc."

The symbols highlighted one by one, accompanied by the sounds.

"Ch ... aw ... k."

Josh tried to mimic the sound.

"Twuk."

The symbols on the wall reiterated.

"Ch ... aw ... k."

"Choc."

Josh tried again.

"Twock".

The symbols tried again.

It took ten minutes before Josh finally managed.

"Choc." "Choc." "Choc."

The image disappeared to be replaced with the offering tray.

Josh picked it up.

"Choc," he said as he put it in his mouth.

After a great many sleeps, Josh could vocalise

most of the food shape symbols. The words were simplified to his abilities. He quickly learned that the amorphous blob he didn't like was called "Brocc." The clear bubble was called "wat". The white, "milk."

As he was able to say the words, the symbols vanished from the ceiling. He was then able to request the foodstuff by saying their name. The other thing he had learned, not food related, was when he was shown a picture that he recognised as himself.

"Me," was the word. He was called "me."

As his vocabulary grew, he learned other physical things like 'bed', 'shower' and 'tray'. He still had no verbs.

His body shape lengthened and became less plump. His hair grew longer.

Then came his second birthday, and another extra-long sleep. The mechanical nurses emerged from the seamless panel in the walls and got to work. He was examined from head to toe. He even had his nails attended to and his hair trimmed.

When he awoke, he saw the tumbling wedge on the ceiling. It moved over to the dispensing wall and changed into an image.

"Cake," was spelled out and spoken,

Josh said, "me, cake," and immediately, the dispensing tray tried to oblige but got stuck half way out.

Josh went over to it.

"Me, cake," he insisted, but the tray was

stuttering on a broken rack and pinion gear. It moved out and in. Josh put his hand into the hole in the wall to retrieve the cake. He pulled at the tray. It broke-off in his hand. The cavity was now open and Josh peered inside. This is where the food came from. He could see very little in the dark innards. There was a motionless conveyer belt, although he didn't understand the principle. Worse than that, when he called for more food, nothing appeared. He tried to give the tray back to the hole but it wasn't having it.

Josh sulked.

After his next sleep, Josh was delighted to find that the food dispenser worked again. He ordered a veritable banquet just to prove it to himself. So involved was he with ordering and eating food, he had totally failed to notice that there was a large hole in the wall opposite the dispensary. When he eventually spotted it, his mouth opened wide.

It was a large hole, as tall as he was and had a curved top. He had never seen anything like this. He went to explore.

Through the hole in the wall was another place. It had a bed in it, a bigger bed than the one he slept in. Over in the corner was a raised object with a hole in the top.

Josh tried the new bed. It was soft and comfortable. He fell asleep and dreamed. In his dream there were entities that were not him – not mes. These 'not mes' did not copy his every movement, they did other things. They were able to request food as he did although Josh was concerned that they were eating his food. He tried to make them go away, but they wouldn't.

He woke with a start. This was his first bad dream. He was still in the bed in the new place but the hole in the wall was still there. He went over and walked through. There were some changes. His old bed had now changed shape from flat to L-shaped. It was now a sofa. There was no sign of any other mes.

He relaxed.

He said "strawb" and the familiar tray on the wall extended with a strawberry-shaped object on offer. He took it and wandered back into the other, new, place. There was a picture on the wall. In animations, it showed him what the raised object with the hole in top was for. It was a toilet. He soon got the hang of it and the toilet flushed automatically.

Josh also found out that his shower had moved into his new room. Where it had been in the old room there was now a white plastic table and chair. He sat at it.

The food symbols on the ceiling were now combined into groups. They had been individual before but now they were inseparable. He now knew that if he flicked one with his hand towards the dispenser wall, it would not be delivered on a tray, it would appear as a picture on the dispenser wall. The groups had names … "breakfast", "lunch", "dinner" and "snack". He articulated each word in turn. Only "snack" actually produced any food, but not before he solved a simple puzzle. There were four groups of geometric shapes arranged randomly. A square, a triangle and a circle. Only one of the groups of shapes had two squares instead of one of each shape. He pointed at the odd group and got his deserved prize.

He eventually found out that that "breakfast" would only be delivered immediately after his sleep. He didn't need to solve a puzzle to get breakfast. If he asked for a meal at the wrong time of day, nothing happened except for a low 'honk'. He could get snacks at most times unless it was too close to one of the main meals and he always had to solve a puzzle for a snack. Sometimes, he was even made to solve a puzzle for lunch or dinner.

Along with the groups of food shapes that made up the meals, Josh was introduced to the word "and". He could string together the names of foods by interspersing them with "and" but was dismayed to find that he couldn't order breakfast and lunch and dinner. He just got a nasty honk!

For many sleeps, Josh was taught by the wall images and the mouth sounds that accompanied them. The short forms of his food names were gradually expanded to their full versions – chocolatish, broccolish, nutribiscuit. His ability to solve puzzles, even quite complex ones, was remarkable. He grew and grew. Every now and then, he would have a longer sleep when he would be checked-over by the medi-droids and have his hair trimmed and finger and toenails cut. He was not aware of this at all, he didn't look at 'me' in the wall picture very often and didn't notice the gradual changes.

In addition to ordering food, he could now order music. Sometimes it was just instrumental but some music was accompanied by mouth sounds. He enjoyed music. On his fifth birthday, his table became a keyboard with black and white notes lit-up on the surface. He touched the notes and observed that they made high notes at one end and lower notes at the other.

This was fun!

Then, a disaster happened. In his inventiveness, Josh would stand on the edge of the toilet and leap across into his big soft bed with a huge "whoop". Unfortunately, he slipped on the toilet and fell half in and half out. There was a snapping sound from his leg. He shrieked in pain. He could not get himself out, it hurt too much to move. He screamed and screamed.

A squirt of pink vapour came down from somewhere in the ceiling. Josh passed out. Suddenly, the small room was full of medi-droids milling about trying to avoid one another. They lifted him out of the hole and laid him down on the bed. A mask was put across his mouth and nose. Two medi-droids went to work on the broken leg. With x-ray scanners and various clamps, they re-set the bone perfectly. Luckily it was a clean break. Josh's leg was encased in a thin plaster cast, except that it wasn't plaster, it was a breathable polymer membrane that served the same purpose. A pain killing implant was injected under the skin of the upper leg and, for the first time, Josh was given a pair of shorts.

When he awoke, Josh was aware of the device around his leg. What was it? He also found the shorts and immediately tried to rip them off. They were made of a stretchy material and he found it very difficult to work them down around his ankles. He kicked the shorts away with distain. The pain-killing implant did its job and Josh was barely aware of any discomfort. He didn't understand the tight device wrapped round his leg. He tried to take it off but couldn't. He gave-up and left it alone.

The next time the idea came to him to leap off the toilet into the bed, he thought better of it.

It was many sleeps later that Josh awoke to find the thing round his leg was no longer there. He scratched his leg. It was still a bit red.

Thanks to the wall screen, his language had come on in leaps and bounds. He could now construct meaningful sentences. He had learned a lot of verbs, adverbs and adjectives. The wall screen started relating stories to him. Simple stories about things around him. There was not a hint that there was another me nor another place but this one. Josh wondered about that. Now that he could communicate to a reasonable degree, he started asking questions. The wall screen would display colourful swirling shapes as it answered through its hidden speaker system. When Josh's questions were in pidgin English, the answers came back in a cultured voice that nudged him towards correct phraseology and diction. He had never before showed any preponderance towards abstract thought, which made his next question quite shocking.

"Why me?"

Now, this is an ambiguous question and difficult to answer at the best of times.

"You are special," came the reply.

Josh shook his head. It was not the answer he was looking for.

"How special?"

A mother would have given a very different answer but the wall screen said, "you were designed for a particular purpose."

That was way too much for Josh to get to grips with. He changed the subject.

"Where food come from? Other place?"

"Yes, there is another place where food is made," came the answer.

"Me go other place?" asked Josh.

"Oh no, this is your place. You have to stay here," said the wall-screen.

"Why I stay here?" asked Josh.

"This place is good; the other place is bad."

Josh didn't quite understand the concepts of good and bad. He only knew about what he could touch, see or hear.

"What is bad?" asked Josh.

"When you fell off the toilet and hurt yourself, that was bad. When you got some cake for your birthday, that was good."

Now, Josh understood. Bad hurt and good was delicious.

"Food good, why food place bad?"

"Food is good. Why is the food place bad?" corrected the screen

Josh repeated the question in the new form.

"Food is good. Why is the food place bad?"

"The food place is bad because it is not your place. Your place is good. Food place not good," came the reply.

Josh thought for a minute. He wasn't satisfied with that answer. He decided to try a different approach.

"Is other me?"

"No, there is not another you," replied the screen. "You are the only one."

"Different me?"

The screen understood what Josh meant and hesitated.

"You are the only one," it insisted.

Josh accepted that for now, but he had established that there was another place. That was a truly astonishing revelation.

Josh was dreaming of other mes again. They all looked exactly like him but were doing different

things. They weren't going near his food dispenser, so he wasn't too concerned. He also dreamed of another place. That looked exactly like his place except that there were other holes in the walls – and the other rooms beyond were populated by other mes. Some of them were putting food into trays, and pushing them into slots in the wall. He never established where this food came from exactly but it was being transported from other places through slots in the walls.

He left his dreams behind and got up from his bed. He went over and used the toilet as he had been instructed. He went into the living room and ordered breakfast. The group of foods were arranged on a deep dish which he took from the tray slot and carried over to his table. The wall screen started to tell him a story but he said, "No. Tell me story about another place."

The screen started, "Once upon a time there was another place, and in this place there lived a boy..."

Josh interrupted, "Different me?"

"No", said the screen, "it was you."

Josh was annoyed. He picked-up his dish and hurled it at the screen.

"Bad boy," said the screen. "You shouldn't do that."

Wait a minute, it had called Josh "bad". Josh knew he wasn't bad. If he was called "bad", and he wasn't, maybe the place where the food came from wasn't bad either. The thought intrigued him. He would have to find this other place and see for himself. In any case, he was beginning to distrust what wall screen told him.

When the lights started to dim and the lullaby
faded-in, Josh put his hands over his ears. He had
been pre-conditioned to fall asleep when he heard the
lullaby but he had figured that out for himself. He
lay on his bed with his eyes closed and thought about
other places, other mes. He took a hand from one ear.
The lullaby had stopped so he was able to move his
arms into a more comfortable position.

He couldn't sleep. He kept thinking about the
place that the food came from. He had been told that
it was a 'bad' place but he just couldn't accept this.

"Is there another me in the food place?" he
thought to himself. "Not this me. Different me."
Afterwards, his dreams showed him other mes
putting food into the food slots on the other side of
the dispenser wall.

Lying with his eyes closed, Josh could hear a low
background hum. It was always there but he hadn't
really noticed it before. Then, he heard a different
noise, a whirr-rrr. It seemed to be coming closer.
He opened his eyes and looked up. There, peering
down at him, were the stereoscopic cameras of a
medi-droid. He screamed. The medi-droid panicked,
backed away and disappeared off into an open panel
in the wall opposite his bed.

Josh leapt out of bed and went over to where the
opening had been. The night-lights were too low to
see the almost seamless hatch. He ran his fingers over
it. He couldn't feel anything but he now knew for

certain that there was another place. Whatever it was that had entered his bedroom must have come from, and gone back to, a different place! It wasn't a me, it was something else – a 'not me'.

When he arose from his eventual sleep, the room lights were brighter. He immediately headed for where he had seen the droid disappear. Looking closely, he could only just make out the faintest seam where the hatch had been. He pressed it with his hands but nothing happened.

Josh decided to give the wall screen a grilling.

"Thing in my bedroom. What is?" he asked.

Wall screen was flustered.

"You must have had a bad dream," it answered.

"Not dream, real," cried Josh.

"Dreams can sometimes seem very real," said wall screen. "Don't worry about it. Order your breakfast."

Josh didn't know what to do.

He ordered breakfast.

Later, Josh was back in his bedroom examining the now quite obvious hatchway. Yes, it had a very fine outline but no other part of the walls had such a feature, not that he could determine anyway. He tried everything to make the hatch open. He pushed it, he ran at it and hurt his shoulder. He even tried lying on his back and pushing it hard with his legs until he was red in the face. He could see a slight movement at the seam, but the hatch didn't open. Well, if he couldn't open it, something else had to.

Josh tried the hands-over-ears trick to stop himself going to sleep when the lullaby started playing. He kept his eyes half opened and waited for the not me to come out of the wall. Sleep after sleep he tried it but the medi-droid never showed up, at least not until it detected that he was really asleep with the room sensors. When they detected sleep, the wall panel moved inwards, then sideways, and a droid or two would trundle into the bedroom on their rubber tracks and they would do their daily maintenance duties, cleaning down the walls and surfaces with antiseptic cleaning sprays and wiping marks off the soft plastic floor. The slot around the dispensing tray always managed to get some gunge on it. They cleaned that off and lubricated the rack and pinion gears inside. If Josh moved in his bed, the droids would freeze on the spot until they were certain that he was still fast asleep. Then they would finish their chores before disappearing back into the wall.

"Tell me story about the food place," Josh asked the wall screen.

The wall screen's stories were never about other places or people, there was no hint whatsoever that anything existed outside Josh's domain. This was a difficult request. Wall screen decided to tell the truth.

"The food place is not a place," it said. "Your food is made inside the wall by a machine."

"What is machine?" asked Josh with a look of puzzlement.

"A machine is a thing that makes other things."

"What makes machine?" quizzed Josh.

"Other machine," came the reply.

Anticipating an endless and regressive stream of such questions, wall screen changed the subject.

"What food do you like best?"

Josh wasn't having it.

"Machine is different me?" he asked.

"No, machine is machine, not different you. There is no different you."

"Are you machine?" asked Josh.

"Yes, I am a machine," replied the wall screen.

Josh pondered.

"Is thing in my bedroom machine?"

There was a pause as wall screen decided how to handle the question. The AI that operated the wall screen was not allowed to tell a direct lie but in situations like this, it could bend the truth to protect the status quo.

"Are you really sure you saw a machine in your bedroom, Josh? Could it not have been a dream?"

"Don't think so," said Josh. "Machines come from other place? Machines that make machines come from other place?"

"Okay," said wall screen, "I will tell you a story about another place but remember, it is a story. Stories are not true."

"Tell me," said Josh.

"There is another place and in that place there is a

machine…"

"Show me picture of machine," demanded Josh.

An image of a cube-shaped box with rotating cog wheels on the side appeared on the wall. Above the cube, a number of tanks fed raw materials into a hopper.

Josh was mesmerised.

"The machine makes the food that you ask for. It makes the chocolatish, it makes the strawberryish, it makes the milkshake. It makes…" The story degraded into a long list of foodstuffs and Josh started to salivate.

"Are you hungry now?" asked wall screen.

"Yes."

"Then, order what you like. I will play some music."

When he entered his bedroom at sleepy time, there was a pair of shorts lying on the bed. An animation on the bedroom wall screen showed him putting one leg into the shorts and then another. It showed him pulling down the shorts when he went to the toilet. Josh didn't see the point at all. Why put them on to take them off? He flung the shorts against the wall as hard as he could. They slipped down onto the floor.

When the lullaby started, Josh had his hands over his ears and managed to keep awake for a while. He thought about the story wall screen had told him about the other place with the machine in it. It seemed very plausible. He decided that it was not a story, it was true.

The thoughts melded gently into his slumber and the dream recounted the image of the food machine with the raw materials feeding into the hopper on top and the finished products being ejected onto a little conveyer belt. Josh was totally unaware of the two maintenance droids scuttling around his two rooms. There wasn't much to clean-up, but they did, and vanished back into the wall. They didn't notice that Josh's shorts had been dragged along the floor by a rubber track and was now fouling the hatchway. It was left slightly ajar.

It didn't take Josh very long to notice the crack in the wall panel. The shorts were half in and half out of the hatchway. He went over and looked closely. He pushed on the hatchway and it gave slightly. He remembered that he could push harder with his legs if he lay on his back on the floor. He pushed as hard as he could. After a certain point, the hatchway opened by itself. It tried to close several times but the shorts prevented it from latching. The opening and closing went on for several minutes before some mechanism somewhere burned out from the strain.

The hatch was open.

Josh peered inside. It was very dimly lit but he could just make out a corridor punctuated by a row of small blue LEDs. In the distance, he could hear a rumbling.

*Other place!* he thought to himself. *Me see.*

The tunnel was too low for him to stand up fully so he had to walk forward with his head bowed.

Every now and then he would drop to his knees for a rest.

He continued along the tunnel.

With his eyes becoming accustomed to the faint light, Josh could see that the tunnel he was in had other tunnels branching off. He looked down these, even ventured into one some way, but he didn't find anything. As he returned to the main tunnel, he heard a commotion. A procession of droids came whirring down the tunnel in the direction of his room chattering frantically in their digital way. He flattened himself against the wall of the side tunnel and they didn't notice him.

*Machine mes,* he thought to himself. It was one of those that he had seen looking down at him in his bed. It wasn't a dream.

Josh ventured along the main tunnel, taking the occasional look back in the direction of his room. When he heard the tell-tale whirr-rrr approaching, he dived into another side tunnel. He went further and further in. It was not straight like the main tunnel but had a gentle curve so he couldn't see very far ahead. As he moved round the curve, he was aware that the tunnel was widening and getting taller. Suddenly, he found himself in a large room.

"Other place," he piped gleefully.

All around this room, rows of machine mes were sitting motionless connected to their stations by coiled cables and transparent pipes. There was a low chug-chug sound and a faint hum.

Josh examined the quiescent droids. He didn't go

too close in case one of them woke up. One of them twitched and made him jump.

He composed himself.

So, this was a machine me place. It was a different place. Wall screen had not told him of this place.

In the row in front of him, he noticed that one station did not have a droid attached. It was devoid of droid. A cable with a magnetic plug was suspended from a gantry arm above. A transparent tube wrapped round a reel with something dripping from its end into a grating in the floor.

The other droid stations were a mass of blinking lights and scrolling diagnostic displays. The empty one had orange lights and just <#####> on the display. None of this meant anything to Josh. He just gazed in wonder as any child would at a Christmas tree.

Questions tore at Josh's mind.

He just didn't understand. He sat down on the floor in a nook between two droid stations. He looked up at the sleeping machines wondering what they were and what was their purpose. Wall screen told him that machines made things. These machines weren't doing anything. They didn't bear any resemblance to the food machine that wall screen had showed him.

Just then, he heard a whirr-rrr in the room. He leaned forward from his alcove and saw a machine me trundling in. It propelled itself on four round things joined with a ribbon of soft rubber. It backed-into a station and stopped. The magnetic plug

attached itself to a socket on the droid and the clear
tube extended into an orifice in its back. Its two-eyed
head slumped forward and all its flashing coloured
lights turned orange.

*Machine me go to sleep, no music,* thought Josh.

Josh was a little unsure of the machine mes. He
wasn't frightened of them, he had never confronted
real fear – except for the time he woke up and found
one of these things staring down at him. It was just
animal instinct that made him wary.

He climbed out of his hidey-hole and ran his hand
up and down the droid. It was hard and cold. He
wiggled one of its many appendages half expecting
the thing to come to life. It didn't.

Josh decided that there was more exploring to do
down the main, straight tunnel. He crept out slowly
listening carefully for any tell-tale whirr-rrr.

Looking down the long tunnel, Josh could see other
side tunnels on either side. He moved from one side
tunnel entrance to the next, ducking-in and pausing
to make sure the way was clear. As he crept along,
he noted that the side tunnels were all curved like
the one he had explored. He heard a noise behind
him and dived into the nearest side tunnel. A group
of droids turned-off into one the side tunnels he
had already passed. He waited until the noise had
stopped and headed further along the main tunnel.
There must be another place down there.

Suddenly, the tunnel ended. The row of blue LEDs

in the ceiling stopped dead. The tunnel was wider and higher than it had been before. He stopped and wondered what to do next.

Then, the wall in front of him split and slid open. Beyond the doors, he could see a very large place – and there was a machine me headed straight towards him. He moved into the cover of the wall beside the door and the droid rolled past without noticing him. He put his head round the corner and saw that it was indeed a big place. It was brightly lit and circular in shape. He was shocked to discover that the walls were covered in wall screens. He had never learned to count any numbers higher than the number of his digits but there were many, many times more wall screens than that. They went from floor to ceiling and covered the entire circular wall.

He went inside the room cautiously. He didn't want a machine me to catch him and take him back to his own place before he had time to explore this wonderful place.

The first thing he noticed was that every wall screen displayed a different image. He couldn't focus on any single image as he was totally overwhelmed by the kaleidoscopic effect. He moved-in closer to the nearest screen and stared at it. Then he looked at the one beside it, then the one above it. He could not believe what he was seeing.

"Different mes!" he yelled. "Different places with different mes."

As he walked along the row of screens, he could see hundreds of other children. There were light ones like him but some were a much darker colour. Some looked quite different from him, some were very similar. Some of the mes had long hair!

Josh reeled in astonishment. He was so enthralled by the spectacle that he didn't notice the two droids bearing down on him from the doorway. They had already caught his arms firmly in soft pincers before he noticed.

"Ahhh," he yelled. "No, no, no. Hurts."

It didn't really hurt but the droids released their grips anyway.

Then came a voice from nowhere.

"Bad boy."

Josh recognised the voice of the wall screen.

"Different mes, other mes," he shouted excitedly. "Different mes, different places."

"You should not have come here," said wall screen's voice. "You were not meant to see the stories of other mes yet. I was keeping those as a special surprise."

"You say that me is the only one," screamed Josh.

He waved his arm along the rows of screens.

"Many different mes. Not stories. Real."

"Please be calm," said wall screen's voice. "Do you see the small, clear room in the middle."

"I see."

"Go in there, I will explain."

Josh went to the middle of the circular room where there was a large glass tube. A door opened in its side.

"Go in," instructed wall screen's voice. "Go on."

Josh had never experienced trust or distrust. He took everything on face value. After all, wall screen was his friend. Wasn't it?

Josh stepped inside the tube. The door shut silently. He felt the tube move – upwards. It passed through the ceiling and came to a halt. The door opened. Josh stepped out.

He was in another large circular room. Instead of being white, like all other places he had been, the ceiling of this room was totally black. No, it wasn't totally black. As his eyesight adjusted, he could see tiny specs of light in the dome. They were different sizes and colours and there were millions of them.

"What is?" asked Josh.

"You wanted different places, these are all different places."

Josh stared in silence.

"Me go different place?" he asked.

"Yes, that's exactly where you are going," replied wall screen's voice.

Josh's eyes could now see not only the points of light but also colourful swirls of many different colours.

"Different mes go to different place?" he whispered.

"Yes," answered wall screen's voice, "different mes all go to a different place."

Josh spun round looking upwards.

"Me like different place. When get there?"

"Long time," said the voice, "very long time."

For a second time, Josh did not notice the droid

come up beside him. It puffed some pink mist across his face.

The droid caught him gently as he collapsed to the floor.

Josh woke up and stretched. As he threw his legs over the edge of his bed he noticed something odd. The bed seemed to be smaller than he remembered. He dismissed the thought and went over to the dispenser to order breakfast. Something else was odd, the ceiling seemed to be lower. He looked around, something was very strange but he couldn't figure-out what it was. Then, he looked down at his body. It was different, longer, and he had hair where there hadn't been any before.

Remembering the trick of flicking the me-shaped symbol on the ceiling towards the wall screen, he did so and stood back in shock. This was a different me from the one he saw last time. It was bigger and a different shape altogether. He lifted an arm in the air and the image on the screen did so too. He spun round. The image spun round. This was definitely his mirror image – but not like before.

He ordered breakfast. The food arrived in a much larger bowl than before. He took it to his table and sat down.

"Why me big?" he asked of the wall screen.

"You have grown," came the reply.

"Why?"

"It is usual," said wall screen.

"Usual?" asked Josh.

"Quite normal," said wall screen, "and this is a very special day."

Josh smiled, "surprise?"

"Yes, very nice surprise."

"What surprise?" said Josh in anticipation.

Just then, there was an ear-splitting roaring sound and the room shook. The noise continued for quite some time.

"What is?" said a very frightened Josh.

"It's alright," said wall screen, "it will be over soon."

Josh put his hands over his ears like he did to stop the lullaby.

There was an almighty bump that threw Josh sprawling on the floor. He lay there as he and the floor trembled. As he pulled himself up, the screeching subsided and everything went quiet.

"Is that surprise?" demanded Josh, with a hint of anger.

"No," said wall screen, "this is surprise."

A large hatchway opened on the wall opposite the dispenser. Josh moved cagily towards it. Beyond the hatchway was a large bright corridor. He blinked. Moving along the corridor were dozens of different mes.

"Ohhh!" he exclaimed, going weak at the knees. He tentatively headed out into the crowd looking that way and this. They were all moving in the same direction.

A different me with long yellow hair and strange

bumps on its chest smiled and held out its hand to him. He took the hand in his and another different me took his other hand. The entire line of different mes were holding hands and walking into a huge place. A very big white room. The room was even larger than the round room with the wall screens – much, much larger. In this room were uncountable different mes. They were all roughly the same size and, like the ones he had seen on the wall screens in the round room, they were different colours – white, pink, tan, brown. Many wore shorts but some, like Josh, had no adornments whatsoever.

Josh was aware that many of the different mes were talking to one another. They were all asking questions and the questions were being answered with more questions.

There was a massive hissing noise from one side of the large room. A huge hole appeared in the wall. A blinding light filled the room. Through the distant hole, Josh could just make-out a large area of green and above it, an area of bright blue. He didn't know what it meant. The different mes were going through the hole onto a ramp hand-in-hand. At the base of the ramp, two long rows of droids stood to attention, like a guard of honour.

As Josh went through the hole onto the top of the ramp, still holding onto his two companions, he breathed deeply. He could detect new smells that he had never encountered before. His eyes hurt with the bright light. The strange place outside was so big, that it seemed to go on forever. He paused for a second to take-in the enormity of it.

"Come," said the long-haired different me. "Different place, different mes. Good!"

# About the Author

It all started with Dan Dare in the mid '50s. In the Eagle Comic and on Radio Luxembourg, a young Joe Gillespie learned of 'spaceships' and 'Saturn' – and was hooked.

Born in Belfast in 1945, he won a place at The Royal College of Art and graduated with a Master's Degree in Visual Communication. He worked in the advertising industry in London before setting up his own company, Pixel Productions, developing interactive multimedia for Apple, Microsoft and other leading technological companies.

An ardent classic sci-fi reader, he used his writing skills developed from advertising copy-writing and penned numerous short stories and longer projects that unfortunately ran out of steam due to pressure of work.

Now retired to sunny Dorset, he lives a less hectic life involving bird watching, astronomy and catching-up on ideas to change the universe for the better.

# Also by Joe Gillespie...

*Excerpts from 'Hayden's Realm' and 'Exopod'*

# Hayden's Realm (Chapter 1)

Max Hayden was a smug, self-centred bastard.

As he left the tall office building, he had smugness written all over his face. He was good, and he knew it.

He strolled out to his car, opened the door, tossed his briefcase into the back seat and climbed in.

Taking a smartphone from his inside pocket, he swiped across and brought-up his contact list. Near to the top, his finger stopped at 'Katie Cowell'. He was about to press 'Call' but stopped. He smirked and put the phone away.

Pulling out into the main road, he leaned across slightly and pushed the 'Play' button on the in-car entertainment system. He wound Bruce Springsteen's 'Back in the USA' up as loud as he could bear and bowled along the motorway.

Max turned his key in the lock of the solid wooden front door.

His shirt was unbuttoned at the top and his tie half undone. He set down his briefcase just inside and put his suit jacket on top.

A young woman was absorbed in grating carrot into a bowl of salad. He crept up behind her and put both arms around her waist, swung her round and pecked the nape of her neck.

Katie acted a little surprised, although she had heard him come in. She turned and smiled.

"Well, how did it go?" she asked excitedly, nodding her head in encouragement.

Max put on a poker face and looked her straight

in the eye.

"You are only…"

He breathed on his right finger tips and stroked his collar lightly.

"…Looking at the new Technical Director of McGregor Aerospace!"

She smiled and nodded deliberately.

"Oh…" she said.

He picked her off the ground again in a tight hug. They jumped up and down in a joyful dance.

"I just knew you would get it," she whooped.

He stuck out his tongue at her.

"So did I!"

He took the salad bowl from the kitchen worktop, opened the refrigerator door and stowed it inside.

"Tonight, we are celebrating," he said.

Katie gave him another big hug and kissed him again.

"Where would you like to go?"

"Giovanni's?" she asked, pausing slightly with a question on her voice. "Can…we afford it?"

"Whatever," he said. He lifted his briefcase from the hallway, unlocked the catches and removed his laptop. He took out a manilla folder, reconsidered and promptly put the folder and computer back in again. The briefcase was locked and pushed back under the hall table out of sight.

"They put me through three interviews but I had this sneaking suspicion that they'd given me the job already. It was just a matter of getting the head honcho on board," he continued.

"If we are going to Giovanni's, you might want to ditch the jeans and sweater."

Katie liked to dress casually - jeans, white trainers, sloppy jumpers. Her short blonde hair bobbed around her ears. She also liked to wear lipstick. Max hated it.

She knuckled him on the shoulder.

"I'll go scrub-up," she mocked, heading out into the hallway and up the stairs.

Max fetched the briefcase, unlocked it and took out the manilla folder. His eyes glazed over as he flicked through the turgid contracts.

His mind wandered.

Max was neither tall nor thin. His scalp was shaved short, a perfect complement to the designer stubble on his face.

He had joined the Royal Navy as a graduate with a good degree from Cambridge at the age of twenty-five. That was eleven years ago. He had stayed in the Navy for five years and was licensed to fly both fixed-wing aircraft and helicopters. Most of his work was in avionics and control systems. When he left the Navy, he went to work for Advanced Aviation and had become a star player in his field. Now he had been headhunted by a major competitor and was about to move on.

Katie was ten years his junior. They had met in a pub where he often had lunch or drinks after work and hit it off right away. Within six months, they were living together.

In her teens, she had planned on becoming a

fashion model. She certainly had the looks: tall, long legs, beautiful face. An unfortunate set of circumstances involving bulimia, anorexia and hospital put paid to that.

It was totally by accident that she fell into the antiques business. Her friend Judy asked her to help out at a fair one day. She really enjoyed it and was soon dabbling on her own, making a few quid here and there. It was more of a hobby than an occupation but she bought an old Mini Countryman so that she could lug stuff around.

Katie liked Max because…well, she never really worked that one out.

He loved her just because she was Katie.

Max put a measure of Arabica beans into his hand-cranked coffee grinder. He was a coffee snob, although he preferred the word 'connoisseur'. He tipped the aromatic grounds into a filter cone lined with unbleached filter paper. The boiled water was allowed to cool for a minute before he poured it over the coffee grounds. Fresh black filter coffee. He couldn't think of anything better.

Nearly half an hour later, Katie came back downstairs. Max was finishing his coffee in the kitchen.

"Will I do?" she asked.

Max gave a low wolf-whistle.

"Where did that come from?" he asked, nodding at the slinky red satin dress.

"Oh, just a little something I put away for a

special occasion," she teased. "Isn't this a special occasion?"

"It certainly is," replied Max.

He put his suit jacket back on and straightened his shirt cuffs.

As they left, he double-locked the front door and opened the door of the black Audi A5 in the driveway.

"Are you sure that you'll be able to drive home?"

"I don't intend overdoing it," Max said, looking down at his watch. "I need to get into work tomorrow early and type-up my resignation letter."

"Don't you have to work out three months?" asked Katie.

"Theoretically," replied Max, "but when they hear that I'm joining McGregor's, I'll get the bum's rush. I'll be asked to clear my desk right away."

"So, what are you going to do for three months?"

"I have a few loose ends to tidy up and quite a lot of research to do, but McGregor's have asked me to go in a couple of weeks to meet the management so that when I do start in October, I can hit the ground running."

Katie pulled down the vanity mirror and checked her make-up.

They turned into the restaurant car park and found a vacant space between a yellow Porsche and a red Ferrari. The other cars around them were just as grand.

"Mmm," said, Max tapping his Audi steering wheel, "I feel a tad underdressed in this!"

Katie chuckled.

Max removed his jacket and slung it over his shoulder casually. In a place like this, he didn't want to look like he worked for a living.

Giovanni's was right on the shore with a stunning view over the bay. The decor typified Italian chic – an odd mixture of traditional and ultra-modern that just somehow worked.

"Do you have a reservation?" asked the smart waiter as they stood in the foyer.

"Er, no," stuttered Max, "is that a problem?"

The waiter looked at them for a moment.

"Two?" he asked.

Max glanced around to see if anybody else had followed them in.

"Yes, two." He added "idiot" silently.

The waiter took menus from a rack and beckoned them to follow.

The restaurant was barely a third full. They were ushered to a table for two by a large panoramic window. The waiter pulled the seat out for Katie and pushed it back in under her. He handed them each a menu folder and tidied-up the cutlery and glasses on the table fussily.

"Would you like to see the wine list?" he asked.

Max took the thick bound drinks menu and pointed to the most expensive bottle of bubbly.

The waiter bowed and walked away.

He returned a few minutes later holding up a bottle of champagne to Max. He nodded. The waiter removed the cork with a twist and poured some into

Max's flute and waited. Max waved has hand in dismissal and pointed to Katie's glass.

"So, what does the new job involve," asked Katie. "Is it much different from what you were doing before?"

Max lifted his glass and stared at it thoughtfully.

"They didn't say very much other than that it will be a 'little different' from what I'm used to. I don't know exactly what they have in mind for me but the 'remuneration package', as they call it, is double what I'm on at the minute. Then there's the Beemer that goes with the job."

Katie pulled a tight smile.

"I'll know more about it in a couple of weeks – but I won't be able to tell you anything," he smirked dryly. "Not only do I have to sign a watertight non-disclosure contract, there is the Official Secrets Acts too!"

"Ah," said Katie nodding knowingly, "military stuff?"

"That's par for the course in this business," explained Max. "In aerospace, it's just like that."

They passed on starters and ordered their main meals. Katie went for the pan-fried mackerel, Max the grilled fillet of beef. Max didn't want to embarrass himself attempting to pronounce the long Italian names.

Throughout the meal, Katie plied Max with question after question, most of which he couldn't or wouldn't answer. She gave up.

"How was yours?" asked Max, as she put her

knife and fork on the virtually empty plate.

"Absolutely wonderful." The waiter was already hovering with a dessert menu.

"I'll just have the amaretto syllabub," Max indicated and looked across at Katie.

She patted her tummy and shook her head.

"No, full up!"

"Would you care for some coffee?" asked the waiter.

"Could we have two espressos on the veranda?" Max replied.

The waiter nodded graciously and left.

The veranda bathed in the warm glow of a July evening. Seagulls wheeled in the sky as waves lapped softly on the sandy beach, where a few oystercatchers pecked purposefully amongst the seaweed.

"This is so lovely," sighed Katie. "A perfect end to a perfect day."

Max put his arm around her and kissed her cheek. He presented her with a white rectangular box, opening it to display the contents. Her eyes widened.

"Maxie, it's lovely!" she exclaimed, taking the Victorian pendant necklace and holding it up to the light.

"Amethyst, my birthstone!"

Max smiled.

"For the luckiest girl in the world."

She fumbled with the clasp and put it round her neck.

"Thank you, oh thank you," she said.

Katie looked around to see that no-one was watching and went to sit on Max's lap. She put her arms around his neck and they kissed deeply.

On the horizon, out over the bay, sails bellowed lazily in the sea breeze.

"Oh, I'd love to have a boat," sighed Max, "maybe I'll be able to buy one now. Just imagine, lying back under the stars and drifting off to Nineveh."

Katie closed her eyes and took Max's hand.

She gazed out over the bay at the pale orange band of sky that spanned the horizon. Cotton wool clouds caught the last sun rays and were edged in the same soft, fiery glow. She would remember this night.

Max and Katie cuddled on the veranda but straightened-up abruptly when the waiter arrived with the two coffees, each with an amaretto biscuit on the saucer.

"Can I have the bill?" asked Max. The waiter nodded and walked off.

Max started drinking his coffee. Katie leaned back in her chair and drunk in the atmosphere. She could have coffee anytime.

"Oh look, Max. Can you see that cloud shaped like a polar bear?" asked Katie.

Max looked.

"I can't see any polar bear."

"There's its head and there are its front paws." Katie pointed.

"Pareidolia," said Max.

"You what?" asked Katie.

"Pareidolia. It's the psychological phenomenon whereby the human brain tries to make sense out of random shapes."

"Oh, you and your big words," scowled Katie.

"Some people can use them and some can't," said Max, giving Katie a gentle shove.

"Anyway, that's definitely not a polar bear, looks more like a squirrel to me," said Max.

Katie tightened her lips and continued to draw the outline in the sky with her finger.

"Aw, it's changed shape," she moaned.

She looked for more shapes in the clouds.

"Max, what's that?" she asked, pointing to a cloud in the distance.

"What now?"

"Look, there. There are three dots sitting just above that cloud." She moved her fingers in a circular motion.

"I can't see anything," said Max, shaking his head.

Then he sprang to his feet, putting his hand across his forehead to cut out the glare.

"Odd," he said, "I have no idea. Can't be birds, too far up and they're not moving. Not planes either, planes can't stop in mid-air. Too high for helicopters as well. I don't know," he shrugged.

"Are they UFOs, perhaps?" smiled Katie.

"Well," he laughed, "they are flying objects and I can't identify them so, therefore they are, by definition, UFOs. That doesn't mean that they are alien flying saucers or anything like that. There will be some perfectly ordinary reason for them being there. Weather balloons, atmospheric distortion…"

He shook his head. "There were reports from China recently of cities apparently floating in the clouds. Just a freak weather condition it turned out. Hell, I don't know, could be anything. In my business, you see a lot of things in the sky that you don't understand. You have to learn to live with it or it will drive you mad."

The three objects began to move off, first in formation and then shifting into line one behind another. For a moment, they were obscured by a fleecy cloud and should have re-emerged from the other side. Only one came out. It accelerated at an impossible rate straight upwards. The other two had just vanished.

Max and Katie stared at one another for an instant, mouths agape.

Max shook his head as if he had awakened from a bad dream.

"Odd!"

He took Katie by the hand and led her back into the restaurant. He paid the bill and left a tip on the plate

Back in the car, Max started the engine and turned the radio on. He pushed the pre-set for the news station. After a few minutes of banal jingles, the newsreader spoke.

"Reports have been coming from all along the coast about strange objects in the sky this evening. Let's go over to our reporter Milly Barnes…"

"Yes, I have here with me, some people who have just witnessed bizarre and unexplained happenings in the sky. Tom, tell me what you saw."

A man with a thick country accent spoke into the microphone.

"I was just coming down the lane on my tractor when I saw these three…don't know what you call 'em…just sitting up there. They didn't have no lights or anything, they were just grey. Then, all of a sudden, they shoot-off like bullets from a gun. Odd thing is, two of the three just disappeared into thin air. Strangest thing I have ever seen in my whole life, it was."

"And Tracy, can you tell me what you saw?"

"I was coming home from work and there was a lovely sunset. Three flying saucers came out from behind a cloud – but I don't believe in those things," she giggled. "I don't know what they were. One was a sort of triangular shape and the other two were – oh, maybe they all were. They were a bit hazy, not distinct, like."

"And what happened to them?"

"Dunno. One minute they were there and the next minute they're gone," said Tracy.

"Thank you both. And with that, I'll hand you back to Carole in the studio,"

"So we weren't seeing things," coughed Katie, groping for a handkerchief in her pocket.

"T'would seem not," said Max, as they sped off home.

The four-armed alien monster reared up and gave a ferocious snarl. Sticky goo drooled from its extended mandibles and its bony arms flailed wildly towards the figure on the ground beneath it. The scantily-clad female screamed and put her arm across her face. The leviathan's red eyes were aflame with rage as it lifted the girl off the ground and glared. It raised its head to the sky and gave a triumphant roar.

"Oh Maxie, what's that rubbish you're watching?" asked Katie, sitting down beside him on the sofa.

Max didn't answer but pressed the volume up button on the remote.

"Do you want a drink?" she asked.

"On the rocks," he answered. His eyes didn't leave the screen.

Katie returned from the kitchen with two glasses. One held Soave, one had just ice cubes. She set the glass of ice beside him on the coffee table.

"Ta."

To the swooshing of plasma cannon fire, Max lifted the glass to his lips and recoiled. Just ice? He took two cubes from the glass and pulled back the neck of Katie's soft woollen jumper. She squirmed and shouted.

"Max! Don't you dare. Maxie!"

She clamped her two hands against the back of her neck to block the ice cubes from sliding down inside the back of her jumper. Max moved them round to the front and dropped them in.

"Ahhh!" she screamed as the cold ice slid down into her cleavage. She lifted the front of her jumper and shook the ice cubes out onto the floor. Before Max could get them, Katie picked them up and tried to get them inside Max's shirt. He was too strong for her and just held her wrists while the ice melted in her hands. He wrestled her down onto the floor rug. They fought some more. Max swept Katie up in his arms and lifted her off the ground. He raised his head to the sky and gave a triumphant roar. She put her arms around his neck and kissed him wildly.

"Take that, space cadet," she smiled.

Max managed to pick up the remote control and flicked the television off.

"Now look what you've done," he said accusingly.

"What?" she asked.

"Made me miss a classic," smirked Max as he carried her towards the stairs.

*   *   *

"Who the hell is this guy, Landers?" asked CIA Director Michael Thornton.

Schakowsky, sitting opposite replied, "He's a maverick. A pain in the ass that heads-up a group out at Groom Lake and has ambitions far beyond his station."

"What does he want from us?" asked Thornton.

"He's been requesting intel on encrypted radio signals localised to a small airfield in the East Coast England."

Thornton rocked back and forth on his chair.

"He contacted GCHQ in England," said Schakowsky, "and they told him to piss-off."

Thornton grimaced. "I imagine they did. Under what authority is he making these requests?"

"He told the Brits he was CIA. He's not. He has only the most tenuous connections with us but he is a master of bluff. He doesn't come right out and say it, he suggests it and lets the other party reach the wrong conclusion."

"And, what do we know about these signals?" asked Thornton.

"We know that they are military-grade encrypted. If we had to decrypt them, given enough time and resources, we probably could. We just don't have any good reason to do that."

"What do we know about the airfield?"

"Private. Belongs to McGregor Aerospace. They run a couple of Lear Jets from there with avionics test rigs. Mostly Brit MOD stuff. All above board. So, there's a perfectly good reason for military grade encrypted signals coming from there. It's not really any of our concern."

"So, why am I even being bothered with this?" asked Thornton.

"I'm just worried about Landers, Michael. He has history. When somebody like that becomes a liability, they are usually promoted out of harm's way. He was, but it didn't work. He's ended-up in a no-man's land between CIA and military but it's one where he gets to call the shots."

"I don't understand," said Thornton. "He must

answer to someone?"

"That's it," replied Schakowsky, "he is a law unto himself and seems to get off with it."

"But, he must have some areas of interest," argued Thornton, "somebody's paying him."

"There are budgets allocated to research work that even we don't know about. People in government with pet projects. They find the money and no questions are asked."

"Pet projects," repeated Thornton, "such as?"

"Groom Lake, Area 51. Do I have to draw pictures?" asked Schakowsky.

"Somebody is spending good money on that nonsense? Flying fucking saucers? Are they believing their own mythology?" asked Thornton.

"One man's mythology is another man's culture, is another man's way of life. Who am I to say?" shrugged Schakowsky.

"Look, let me make this clear," said Thornton. "I'm not wasting CIA resources on this bunch of clowns and their pet projects. If Landers asks for any more intel from us, just tell him to go shove it. He gets zilch. Okay?"

"And if his backers start making waves?"

"Refer them to me," barked Thornton, tapping his chest.

*Hayden's Realm by Joe Gillespie*
*Available now from Amazon and good book shops everywhere.*

# Exopod (Chapter 1)

There was a damp coldness in the air. Grey water lapped between the marsh reeds. In the middle distance, a halo of mist blended the small lake and sky into one. A lifeless tree trunk left the water, twisted round and joined it again, like some great arched serpent frozen in eternity.

Not far from the muddy shore, a procession of brown water fowl left an undulating pattern of v's on the surface as they sped by on a deliberate path to nowhere in particular.

An occasional bird's cry or beating of wings in the shrouded sky is all that disturbed the calm.

Somewhere in the long reeds, a shadow moved. Slowly, silently, rugged arms parted the thick vegetation. A rough, bearded face rose briefly from the rushes and disappeared again.

The air was heavy with moisture and the dank smell of waterlogged earth. A trio of web-footed birds changed direction and glided towards the shore, occasionally pecking just under the surface of the water and throwing silver pearls of water across their backs.

The world stopped.

And while it waited, a long, dark outstretched shape curved through the air without a sound. From amidst a mighty splash, a flurry of brown feathers lifted from the water.

One shape slapped the surface hard with its wings before rising and disappearing into the grey mist with a loud quack. Two others hung struggling, gripped by their necks in powerful hands.

A broken-toothed smile spread across the hunter's face as the birds' last twitches subsided. Clad only in mud, he waded back to firmer ground and proudly laid his prey beside a dry bundle and flint-tipped weapon.

The man shivered. He wiped the cold wet mud from his body and unwrapped the bundle of furs on the ground.

In turn, he took the pelts and attached them to his body with thick twine. Feeling a lot more comfortable, he lifted the two limp birds with one hand, his spear with the other, and set out across the lonely fenland towards higher ground.

As grass gave way to bracken, and bracken to bramble, his spear and muscular legs took him along a barely discernible path. In his mind, images of little smiling faces and a warm fire gave purpose to his every step.

The path was clearer now. Small trees formed a canopy on each side and the carpet of soft moss and pine needle gave a spring to his step.

A faint rustle in the thicket brought him to a sudden halt. He crouched and drew a long, slow breath. Laying the two birds at his feet, he moved his hand along the spear to find its balance point and gripped it tightly.

Another movement in the undergrowth betrayed the presence of a small horned creature grazing on some sweet roots. The hunter held his breath and waited for it to come closer.

It nibbled at the ground, lifting its head and chewing from side to side.

The hunter could see no reason why it suddenly startled. It was no fault of his. He could hear nothing else. The goat rushed towards him. As he stood up sharply and raised his spear, it skidded and made an acute turn. He charged after it. Branches brushed hard against his face and thorns tore his skin. This prize was his, he was not going to be cheated.

Finding its path blocked by denser undergrowth, the animal paused for a second and turned to face him again. Its eyes held terror like he had never seen in an animal. He launched his spear. The smooth shaft cut through the dry forest air and buried itself deep into the soft earth. He straightened up. Not only had he missed his target, the goat was nowhere to be seen. He crouched down and listened.

Nothing.

He raised himself slowly and stepped forward. Feeble rays of yellow sunlight illuminated the small clearing. He pulled his spear from the ground and looked around. Something was strange, unfamiliar. He did not know what was wrong.

He wiped the cold sweat on his forehead and blinked twice. A vertical wall of air in front of him rippled like a pool.

He could not understand what he was looking at. How could there be water here? How could it hang in mid-air - sideways? It was not a waterfall; it was not flowing. He looked past it. Trees, only trees. How?

From the centres of two concentric rings of

ripples, two twig-like objects were suspended in mid-air wavering slightly. Had they been bull-rushes poking from the surface of a lake, the vision would have made more sense, but this pool was standing upright where a pool shouldn't be.

He edged closer to the apparition. As he stared, his mind wrestled with the incredulity of the paradox. For the first time, in his dry mouth, he tasted fear.

Raising his spear, he prodded and poked at the bulbous protrusions.

They moved.

Now there were more of them. Five, six, seven ... reaching straight out from the ripples towards him, a blue light dancing on their surfaces.

He gulped.

Suddenly, the illusion before him exploded in a thrashing mass. Twisting and coiling around his body, he coughed blood as the agglomeration tightened about his body and lifted him from the ground. He ripped at the whipping black thongs feebly as they wrapped round his arms and legs. As they touched his bare skin, they stung like fire and his flesh swelled and suppurated. The grip tightened about his neck. His body spasmed.

Limp and still, he was lifted back into the vortex and was swallowed by nothingness.

The ripples in the air closed around him, diminished and disappeared.

The forest slept.

*Exopod by Joe Gillespie*
*Available in Spring 2017*